THE INVISIBLE DAUGHTER

Victorian Romance

FAYE GODWIN

Tica House
Publishing

Copyright © 2019 by Faye Godwin

All rights reserved.

No part of this book may be reproduced in any form or by any electronic or mechanical means, including information storage and retrieval systems, without written permission from the author, except for the use of brief quotations in a book review.

PERSONAL WORD FROM THE
AUTHOR

Dearest Readers,

I'm so delighted that you have chosen one of my books to read. I am proud to be a part of the team of writers at Tica House Publishing. Our goal is to inspire, entertain, and give you many hours of reading pleasure. Your kind words and loving readership are deeply appreciated.

I would like to personally invite you to sign up for updates and to become part of our **Exclusive Reader Club**—it's completely Free to Join! I'd love to welcome you!

Much love,

Faye Godwin

FAYE GODWIN

VISIT HERE to Join our Reader's Club and to Receive Tica House Updates:

https://victorian.subscribemenow.com/

PART I

CHAPTER 1

Fae had never seen so much green before.

She barely heard the crowd around her. Compared to what she was used to on the streets of London, this was nothing; just a handful of travelers stepping out onto the platform, talking, jostling her tiny figure as she stood among them—a lonely six-year-old clutching obediently to her little bag in one hand and her dolly in the other.

Instead of looking out at the chaotic streets of London, she was captivated by the landscape beyond the little train station. The great, long sweep of pure green hillside rolled away to the bottom of the valley, where a group of houses sat companionably together like old friends at a tea party; then the hills beyond, and the hills further beyond that still, all were a patchwork of fields and farmlands bordered with hedges and gray stone walls. It looked like the painting that hung in Mama's living room, but Fae hadn't known a place like this really existed. She had thought it was a painting of heaven.

She had asked her mama about it once. "Mama, which part of heaven is that?"

"It's not heaven, Fae." Mama's voice, as usual, was tired. "It's where your grandparents live."

"I have grandparents?"

"Everyone has grandparents."

Mama didn't want to talk any more about it then. But now, Fae was about to meet them. Thinking about her grandparents made her stomach clench with fear. She tried not to think about it, staring up instead at the sky. It was so blue; there was no smoke in it, not even a cloud, just a great expanse of vast space that made her tremble a little. Even the air was different here. It tasted cleaner somehow. Maybe this really was heaven. Maybe she didn't actually have to be afraid.

But she was afraid. And she missed her mama. And almost more than anyone, she missed Edith, even though it was Edith who had started all this trouble.

❦

She remembered the day that Mama had first told

her about Edith, only they hadn't known then that her name would be Edith, or even that she would be a girl. She hadn't been a person at all yet. She was just a bulge: a swelling in Mama's belly as Mama sat cross-legged on the bed, slowly rubbing her hands over her skin, which looked like it had been stretched as tight as a drum because of what was growing inside.

Fae's little hands were on Mama's belly, too. She wanted so badly to feel the baby kick. Mama said that sometimes the baby would move, and you could feel it. It was still hard for Fae to believe there was a real baby inside that bulge in Mama's belly, but if she could just feel the baby move, then perhaps she'd know it was real. She wanted a brother or sister so badly. Sometimes when she stared out of the windows and into the street, she saw children playing together with their brothers and sisters, and it looked wonderful. Fae had never played with other children before. Perhaps this baby would be her first real friend.

She didn't say this to Mama, though, because she knew it would only make Mama sad. Instead, she asked, "Is it a baby sister or a baby brother, Mama?"

"We don't know yet, darling," said Mama. There was a glow behind her eyes as she smiled at Fae, something that Fae had never seen before. "We'll know when the baby comes out."

"How does the baby get out?"

Mama kissed Fae's forehead. "By magic, my dear," she said.

"What will it look like?"

"We don't know yet. Perhaps a little like me. Perhaps a little like you," said Mama, reaching out to touch Fae's cheek. "All babies are beautiful in their own way."

"I hope it's a baby girl," said Fae. "I'd love a brother, too, but I really want a sister. We can play together."

"That's right, love," said Mama, laughing softly. "You'll be able to play together, and we'll be a real family." Her eyes grew misty with longing.

The mention of family reminded Fae of the man. He didn't live with them, but she knew he and Mama were like the other pairs of men and women walking around on the street together. Except that the man and Mama didn't go outside together. He called her his favorite secret, and Fae wasn't sure if Mama liked being his favorite secret or not. "Will he like this baby, Mama?" she asked.

Mama didn't ask who Fae was talking about. There was only one *he* in the small circle of their lives. "You don't need to worry about him," she said. "Don't think about him, love."

"But he's never liked me," said Fae. "What if he doesn't like the baby, either?"

"Please, Fae." Mama sighed. "Just don't worry about him." Her voice relented a little as she gazed down at her belly, at Fae's tiny hands in between her bigger ones. "He will like this baby," she said softly. "It's his baby, after all."

Fae cocked her head to one side. "Then how come I'm not his baby, too?"

"Oh, Fae, why are you asking so many difficult questions today?" Mama moaned softly.

"But why aren't I, Mama? Did I do something wrong?"

"No. No, you didn't." Mama pulled Fae into her arms. "It's just that he's not your papa."

"Then who is my papa?"

A grim veil came down over Mama's face, transforming her sweet, smooth features to stone. She didn't reply, and Fae knew it would be useless to try to get anything out of her now. Instead, she tried something else. "If he's not my papa, is that why he hates me so much?" she whispered.

She thought she saw a tear gleaming in Mama's eye, but before she could be sure, Mama suddenly got up. "Come on," she said, grabbing Fae's hand. "Let's go and get supper ready."

※

WHEN THE BABY WAS BORN AT LAST, IT WAS A LITTLE GIRL, and Mama named her Edith. Fae got to call her a sister, even though they didn't have the same papa. Edith was soft and cuddly and smelled like lavender and talcum powder, and Fae loved her more fiercely than she had ever loved anything before. Mama said she was too little to carry her baby sister, but she always used to sit in her favorite big, warm armchair with Edith cradled in her arms, and then Fae was allowed to climb up into her lap and play with the baby. Edith's games consisted mostly of grabbing at Fae's fingers with chubby little hands and squealing in delight. The baby had dark blue eyes and a tuft of brown hair right on the top of her head, and even though there were no teeth in her smile, it was the most beautiful thing that Fae had ever seen.

She was sitting in Mama's lap one night, playing with the baby, when they heard a key turn in the lock of the front door. Only one person ever came through that door, and Fae knew she had to get out of his way. She slipped down off Mama's lap and scampered across the room to hide behind the couch on the far end of the room, but even as she lowered herself into the cobwebby dusk, she knew she was too late. The man had spotted her.

She peered around the edge of the couch as he stepped into the room, his eyes resting on her. They were cold and gray, and they made Fae tremble, knowing that he was about to shout and pull her out from behind the couch and kick her out of the room – literally, his big boots slamming into her back.

Instead, the man seemed content with just glaring. He turned to Mama instead, and when his eyes rested on the baby, they warmed.

"Hello, my beautiful secret," he said, coming over to Mama.

She tipped up her chin obediently and he leaned down to kiss her, quickly, tenderly. Then, he gazed down at the little baby. Fae held her breath. What if Mama was wrong? What if he didn't like the baby, and he wanted to kick or slap her, too? But when the big man's fingers reached down toward Edith, she gurgled and held out her hands, grabbing at him. To Fae's astonishment, he gave a deep laugh. She'd never heard him laugh before.

"Isn't she beautiful?" Mama whispered. "She has your lips."

"And your eyes, my love," said the man. He tenderly caressed Mama's cheek. "She is lovely. May I?" He held out his arms.

Mama hesitated for just a moment, clutching Edith close to her chest. Then, relenting, she held the baby out, knowing that his asking was nothing more than a courtesy.

The man scooped Edith up into his hands. Her tiny body, little more than a doll, rested easily in both of his great hands. He gave a booming laugh. "Look how perfect you are," he said. "What a little miracle."

Fae felt her heart crack at his words as she peered out from behind the couch. What was so wrong with her, that nobody ever spoke to her that way? Nobody called her perfect, or beautiful, or a miracle. She knew Mama cared for her, but she always felt like she was a little in her mother's way. If only someone would look at her the way the man was looking at Edith.

If only she had a papa, too.

A VOICE CALLING OUT HER NAME JERKED FAE FROM HER reverie and back to the platform where she was standing now. She blinked, looking around, suddenly feeling lost and bewildered. Mama and Edith were so far away – she'd been on the train for hours. She turned, searching for a familiar face somewhere, but she was drowning in a sea of strangers. Her heart hammered against her chest. Suddenly the blue sky wasn't such solace anymore; she wanted her mama, she'd never been more than a wall's breadth away from her mama before, and now she was completely alone. Clutching her dolly, she looked around wildly. She needed to hide. She needed to find a place to hide before someone saw her.

"Fae!"

The voice came again, but Fae didn't recognize it. She backed away, eyeing the space underneath a nearby cart. She could run and hide in those shadows until the world made sense, until Mama came back for her. But as she started in that direction, a whip cracked; with a snort, the mule hitched to the cart jumped forward, and it drove away. She felt naked and exposed on the bare earth, like a hapless ladybug on the London pavement, about to be crushed underneath a cartwheel.

"Fae!"

There was nowhere to hide, so Fae just froze. Through the crowd, she saw an elderly couple heading toward her. The old lady was a few steps ahead of the old man; even though she walked with a cane, she seemed sprightly. She had a lorgnette in the other hand, and when she spotted Fae, she stopped and raised the glasses to her eyes.

"Fae? Fae Carter?" she demanded.

Fae was far too afraid to respond. She just stared up at the old lady, trembling slightly, as she leaned closer. An old man – her husband, Fae assumed – shuffled up behind her. He was wheezing and his white hair was escaping from under his cap.

"Well, child?" demanded the old lady, studying her with sharp green eyes from behind the lorgnette. "Don't you know your own name?"

"There's a label," offered the old man.

Fae looked down at the label Mama had tied to her jacket with a piece of string. She couldn't read the letters that were written on it, but maybe the old lady could, so she took it off and held it out silently. The old lady's eyes seemed to barely brush the label before she snorted and stuffed it into her pocket.

"It *is* you," she said. "What a scrawny little scrap you are – although we could hardly have expected any better, considering..." Her eyes darted around the platform as if she were afraid someone might have heard what she was saying.

Fae didn't know what to do. "Are you my grandma?" she asked softly.

"Yes, I suppose I am," said the old lady with a sigh. "Well, come along, then." With that, she turned on her heel and walked briskly away, her cane clicking on the platform with each step.

Fae was still frozen solid with fear. The old man shuffled a little closer and reached out with a gnarled old hand to take the bag Fae was still clutching. "Come on, little one," he said, holding out his free hand. "There's nothing to be afraid of."

Fae stared up at him. His eyes were deep blue, the same color as Mama's, and they held a warmth that Fae hadn't expected. She wanted to trust him. Reaching out, she gripped his wrinkled hand.

"Reginald!" shouted Grandma. "Do come along!"

"Stick close to me," said Grandpa, winking. "We don't want you getting run over on your first day out in the country, do we?"

Fae nodded mutely, and Grandpa shuffled off in Grandma's angry wake as best as he could. Fae clung tightly to his hand, but as they left the platform behind, she looked back over her shoulder at the railway that was laid out as straight as a ruler, reaching across hill upon hill to the distant horizon. She fancied she could see some smoke in the air that way; perhaps it came from the factories she'd seen in London. Perhaps Mama was looking up at that same smoke right now.

Or perhaps that train had taken her to an entirely different world. A world she didn't know.

A world that frightened her.

CHAPTER 2

They rode to Grandma and Grandpa's house in a little cart drawn by an old donkey that didn't seem able to go as fast as the horses had always gone back in London. He was a shaggy creature with tiny hooves, long hairy ears, and a very small, very white, and very soft nose. In fact, Fae wouldn't even have known what he was – she had never seen a donkey before – if Mama hadn't shown her a picture in a book of Jesus going up to Jerusalem on the donkey. Mama said that donkeys had black crosses on their backs because of that day, and where Fae sat close beside Grandpa on the driver's seat of the cart, she could see the shape sketched across the donkey's back like a shadow.

"Mama said that donkeys have crosses because of Jesus," she said, looking up at Grandpa.

"Hush, child," snapped Grandma. "There's no need to draw more attention to yourself than necessary." Her grandmother glanced nervously over her shoulder, even though the roads had been completely empty for several minutes since leaving the train station.

Grandpa smiled at her, though. "Did she, then?" he said. "That's very true."

"I'm surprised your mama even remembers who Jesus is," muttered Grandma.

Fae didn't know what that meant. She decided not to ask; Grandma was so scary with her lorgnette and her angry eyes—cold as pebbles on the bottom of the Thames. Instead, she gazed around at the fields and woods that were all around them as the donkey slowly clip-clopped along.

There were farmlands with little green plants just sprouting up in them in neat rows; woolly sheep grazing on the hills, and a herd of horses that startled when they heard the donkey cart and galloped off madly. That made Fae laugh in wonder. She'd never seen horses running like that before, only laboring away between the shafts of some vehicle.

"Look, Fae." Grandpa took a hand off the reins to point ahead. "There's your new home."

"No," snapped Grandma, "that is *our* home." She glared at Fae. "You will be a guest."

Fae looked in the direction Grandpa was pointing. The white-washed cottage was as pretty as the painting in Mama's room; its windowsills and doorframes were all painted blue, and there were window-boxes with all sorts of plants, and something was growing up one of its walls that bloomed with bright purple flowers. Towering behind it, dwarfing the little house with its height and stature, was a great old oak tree. It was the biggest tree Fae had ever seen, and something about it seemed to call to her.

"I like the tree," she whispered.

"I like that tree, too, poppet," said Grandpa. "Your great-great-great-great-great grandfather planted it there in that garden." His voice was filled with love and pride. "This farm has belonged to your family for many generations."

"Don't be so familiar with the child, Reginald," snapped Grandma.

Grandpa didn't say anything. He just brought the donkey to a halt. Fae half tumbled off the cart, clutching her bag and dolly, and Grandpa climbed off stiffly to help Grandma down. "Go on ahead, dear," he told Fae.

"But don't touch anything!" snapped Grandma.

Holding her dolly tightly to her chest, Fae moved on ahead. The front door swung open to her touch, and the kitchen was filled with the warm scent of fresh bread. Fae could see two loaves sitting on the kitchen table, covered with a checkered blue dishcloth. But she wasn't interested in the kitchen. She was interested in the greenery beyond, glimpsed through the glass pane in the back door. Tossing down her bag, she ran through the kitchen and out through the back door, and it seemed like paradise was lying there waiting for her beyond.

This was the best view of them all. The long, smooth expanse of the lawn ran up to meet the feet of the mighty tree; its shady branches spread over the house and the rest of the garden like the sheltering wings of a mother hen. The sunlight seemed different here than in the rest of the world – greener, purer somehow, as if the leaves of the great tree had filtered its impurities. And beyond that was the vegetable garden in all its messy glory, and beyond that was a little road and then a great sweep of hillside running up, filled with purple-blooming heather, to meet the sky.

Laughing, Fae threw the door wide open and ran outside, her bare feet tangling with the fresh grass. She ran all the way to the tree and threw her arms around it as if it were an old friend. Pressing her face against the bark, she felt its roughness, its power, and she loved it.

"You! Child! What do you think you're doing?"

Grandma's shriek shattered the peace. Frightened, Fae backed away, clinging her dolly closely to her chest. "I – I was just..." she stammered out.

Grandma stood in the back door, her eyes flashing like struck flint. "Come inside right now!" she ordered.

Obediently, Fae ran into the house, ducking under Grandma's arm. The old lady smelt of mothballs. When Fae was safely in the kitchen, she slammed the door shut and turned angrily to Fae.

"You are not to go outside during the day – *ever*," she said. "You will only go out when I tell you. Do you understand? You shall not be seen. I won't have your mother's shame on my head."

Before Fae could ask any questions, Grandma stomped off, disappearing upstairs. She realized that there were tears in her eyes. Clutching her dolly, she sank down to the cold kitchen floor, staring longingly out of the backdoor's window at the great tree that had made her feel so overwhelmed with joy for such a short time.

"Come on, pumpkin." It was Grandpa. He laid a hand on her shoulder. "Don't cry."

Fae struggled to her feet and wiped her nose, encouraged by his gentle tone. "May I never, ever go outside, Grandpa?" she whispered.

"No, darling, it's not that bad. You're allowed outside sometimes," said Grandpa, smiling down at her. "Early in the mornings before everyone starts to work, and late in the evenings when all the work is done, you may play outside. And every Sunday morning when your grandmother and I have gone to church."

"Church?" asked Fae.

Grandpa took a deep breath, and sorrow crossed his face. "Your grandma believes church is a place to show everyone how much better she is than they are," he said with deep sorrow in his voice. "For me, I think it's a place where you go to find healing."

"But why don't I get to come to church?" asked Fae. "Look." She pulled up her dress. "I bumped my knee. I want healing, too."

"Church heals a different kind of hurt, love," said Grandpa. "At least, it does if you let it." He stroked her hair. "I wish you could come."

Grandma poked her head back through the doorway. "No, Reginald," she snapped. "That little urchin may under no circumstances come to church with us. Can you imagine what the people would think?" She shuddered visibly. "The daughter of a – of a..." She shook her head. "I don't even want to say it."

Grandpa sighed. "I'm sorry, Fae," he said, quietly enough that Grandma couldn't hear. "You can't come because your grandma and her friends don't approve of your mother. They would be unkind to you. It's best you stay here, where you're safe."

"But Mama is wonderful." Fae raised her voice, anger rising in her. "I love my Mama. She's the best person I know!"

"Ha," Grandma's snort cracked like a whip in the air. "You're proof that she isn't, aren't you?"

"Theodora!" gasped Grandpa.

A brief look of regret crossed Grandma's face, but she said nothing; she just stormed out. Fae just looked down at her feet, knowing Grandma was right. There was something bad and wrong about Fae, something she didn't understand, but it still ate at her heart. She didn't mean to be a mistake, but she knew there was something wrong with her. That was why Mama always used to hide her away.

***

Mama's favorite place to hide Fae and Edith had always been inside the little kitchen. It was small – containing a little table, some cupboards, and a squat coal stove with a little metal chimney – almost too small to prepare meals in, and certainly too small for two little girls to try to keep themselves entertained. Especially when one of those little girls was barely crawling and had a tendency to be loud.

"Shhh, Edith!" Fae hissed for the thousandth time that evening. She grabbed her baby sister's hands, stilling them so Edith couldn't shake her rattle. "You need to be quiet now."

Edith howled angrily, shaking her little fist. Fae hurriedly let her go – the sound of the rattle was better than her whining.

"Please, Edith," she begged. "Hush now. You can't fuss now."

THE INVISIBLE DAUGHTER

Edith shook the rattle a couple of times, but this didn't seem to appease her. She dropped it on the floor and crawled over to the kitchen door. Using the doorframe to support herself, she dragged herself to her feet and reached for the handle. When it proved to be several feet higher than her extended hand, she started to whimper.

"No!" Fae hurried over to her, pulling her away from the door and into her arms. "Edith, shhh!"

"Ma-ma-ma-ma!" whimpered Edith, her baby lips flapping loosely around the sounds. "Mama!"

"I know you want Mama," Fae whispered in Edith's ear, rocking her gently to and fro. She was aware that her hands were shaking uncontrollably. "Mama's busy with him now. You can't have her right now. You just have to be quiet for a little while, until they're done."

But Edith would not be placated. She raised her voice even higher, reaching a shrill pitch that sliced through Fae's ears. "MAMA!" she howled. "MAMAAAAAAA!"

"Edith!" Fae clapped a hand over the baby's mouth. "Be quiet!"

In response, Edith gave an ear-piercing shriek that rang around the kitchen as she slapped Fae's hand away. There was a yell from upstairs, and Fae heard footsteps storming down the stairs, a door slamming. She grabbed Edith, not caring now that the baby was screaming at the top of her lungs and dove under the kitchen table.

It was no good. Before Fae could find a better place to hide, the door banged open, and the man stood in the doorway. His chest was heaving, his face scarlet; he had no shirt on, and his hair was in disarray, flopping over his flashing eyes.

"Cursed children!" he thundered. "You were told to be quiet!" He lunged toward them. "I'll show you how to be quiet!"

"No!" screamed Fae, clutching Edith's little dress. The baby gave a scream of absolute terror as the man's hand closed like a vice around her tiny arm. Fae clung to the fabric, but it was ripped out of her fingers as the man hoisted Edith high in the air, dangling her by one arm. Edith's mouth was wide, her face red and wrinkled as she howled in fear, her cries and screams reverberating around the room.

"No! Put her down! Give her back!" screamed Fae, running forward, her arms extended toward Edith. "You're hurting her! Let her go!"

She rushed toward him, and his foot flashed out, catching her hard in the stomach. She skidded across the slippery floor, coming to a halt on her side against a kitchen cupboard. Heedless of the pain in her stomach, she scrambled to her feet, her eyes still fixed on Edith. The baby's screams reached a deafening pitch.

"Put my sister down!" shrieked Fae.

"Please." Mama had appeared behind the man, clutching her shift around her. She touched his arm. "Please, don't hurt her. Give her to me."

Her voice was a faint, weak, trembling thing, pale and pathetic in the face of Edith's screams. But it seemed to work. The man relented slightly, swinging Edith angrily toward Mama. She grabbed the baby and tucked her into her arms, pressing Edith's face into the crook of her neck. Her muffled cries stilled, and an appalled silence settled over the room except for the faint sniffling as Edith cried into her mother's bosom.

The man's chest was heaving with effort. He turned back to Fae, and the expression he gave her was terrifying. It was murderous and uncontrollable, a ravaging pack of wolves on the hunt for helpless prey, ready to rip out their throats. It made Fae cower in the corner, and when he turned on Mama, she did the same, backing away as she clung to Edith.

"That child has never been anything but a nuisance," he spat in Mama's face. "If I had known you were with child when we first met, I would never have kept you."

Tears were pouring freely down Mama's cheeks. She whispered, "Please," so quietly that Fae didn't hear it, just saw her mouth around the shape of the word.

"You had better get rid of that nuisance." The man jabbed an accusing finger toward Fae. "I don't ever want to see her again. See to it that she isn't here when I come next – or there will be consequences." His voice lowered dangerously. "Remember that I could always send you back to where you came from."

Terror filled Mama's face. She shook her head wildly, clinging more tightly to Edith.

"See to it," spat the man. "I want her gone."

He stormed away, and Mama's knees seemed to buckle. She slid gently to the ground and sat there, her shoulders shaking as she sobbed, holding her baby so tightly that Edith was beginning to moan again. As soon as the door slammed behind the man, Fae crawled over to her, too scared to stand up and walk.

"What's wrong, Mama?" she begged, stroking her mother's face, her hair, her hands. "What's the matter? Tell me what's wrong, Mama. What's wrong? What is it?"

But Mama never told her.

Sunday mornings became Fae's favorite time out in the country. It was so boring inside the big house; Grandma was always busy churning butter or baking bread or knitting something, and she shouted at Fae if she made any sounds or ran around. Fae was good at staying quietly in a small room, but it was worse without Edith around her. She missed her terribly.

The worst times were when Grandma had friends to visit her. They would stay for hours, clustered around a table in the parlor, gossiping away while Fae had to stay locked securely in her room for the whole day long, not allowed to make a sound. Grandma told her that she had to hide or her friends would all turn into wolves and eat her up. She didn't quite believe this, but she was more afraid of Grandma than of a thousand wolves, so she did it anyway.

Every day, when Fae opened her eyes and saw just a chink of light through the curtains, she'd run outside and play in the big tree or roll around on the lawn with her dolly. It would only last a precious hour before Grandma would call her in again, but it was something. She also loved the brief time she was allowed out in the evenings.

But Sundays, oh, Sundays were glorious. Sometimes Grandma and Grandpa would be gone for three or four whole hours, and Fae spent every moment outside on that lawn. She built little cities and houses out of sticks and acorns for her dolly; she dug in the dirt, she gathered different shapes and colors of leaves, but her favorite thing of all was to climb the big tree. It had low-hanging branches that were easy to get onto, and from there she could scramble up so high that she felt she might fly away like a little bird into a different life.

The first day that Fae spoke to the boy with the glasses was a beautiful, perfect, summery Sunday morning. Not a single breeze even stirred the leaves of the great tree; it only rustled where Fae touched it as she climbed up to the highest branch that she'd dared to go to. With an effort, and almost tearing her dress, she made it to the branch. Lying on her belly, she used her arms and legs to tug herself forward until she reached a patch of dappled sunshine. It was deliciously warm on her back, and she lay there, allowing her arms and legs to hang down on either side of the bough, to gaze out toward the heather-decked hillside.

Grandpa had told her that the hillside was the common. She often saw children playing there – usually a group of boys. Just as she'd always sat inside her house with Mama and watched the children playing in the street outside, she often sat in her little room and gazed out at the common where all the boys were running around together. Their games looked rather rowdy and wild – hitting each other with sticks and tumbling over each other in mad games of tag that always turned into wrestling – but Fae still wished she could be out there with them. Perhaps she could play with the boy with the glasses. He was smaller than the other boys, and he seemed to like reading; maybe that was why he had to wear little round spectacles all the time. The other boys called him Ollie, even while they were teasing him. But Fae knew she would never play with him; he only ever came out while she was locked inside.

She pressed her cheek into the rough bark, feeling drowsy in the warm sun. If only she could have shown Edith this wonderful place. It would have been so much more fun if Edith had been here. She could just imagine her little sister sitting in the grass, giggling as she felt its rough texture against her chubby legs, digging her fingers into the rich, cool dirt. Maybe one day, when she was big, she would go back to the town and get Edith and they would play underneath this shady tree all day long...

The scuffing noise of a shoe being kicked into the dirt jolted Fae from her daydream. Sitting up, she stared toward the common, and there he was. The sunlight flashed on the surface of his spectacles, but he wasn't looking her way; instead, he was gazing down at his feet as he kicked a pebble along the surface of the road. His hands were pushed deep into his pockets, straining his suspenders, and his straw hat was tipped back on his head. This time, he didn't have a book under his arm as usual, nor was he whistling carelessly. In fact, the slump of his shoulders made him look upset. Was that a tear on his cheek?

Fae leaned closer, trying to see the boy more clearly. It was a mistake. With a loud snap, a twig broke somewhere underneath her left knee. The boy looked up sharply, and Fae felt a stab of terror. She had to run before he saw her. Scrambling down the branches, wild in her haste, she banged her elbow on the rough bark and couldn't care less. Grandma would kill her if she knew she'd been seen.

"Hey! Stop!" the boy called.

Fae had almost reached the ground. She knew she had to get away from him. She tried to jump down from the second-to-last branch and felt a swooping fear in her guts as she realized it was much too far. With a yelp of terror, she threw out her hands and tumbled, hard, into the dirt. A jolt of pain shot up her left arm, and she rolled upright, clutching it. Tears filled her eyes. Her arm throbbed.

She heard running feet, and before she could react, the boy was beside her. He looked down at her with warm, kindly eyes and crouched down next to her. She saw that he was older than she was – maybe eight or nine years old – and the fact calmed her a little.

"You poor thing!" the boy exclaimed, touching her arm lightly. "I'm sorry. I didn't mean to startle you. Are you hurt?"

Fae swallowed her tears. Her arm was feeling a little better, almost as if Ollie had made it better just by touching it.

"A little bit," she said, wiping her nose.

"Well, can you wiggle your fingers?" asked Ollie.

Experimentally, Fae did so. "Yes, I can," she said.

"Oh, that's good. My brother Otis broke his arm falling off his pony last year, and he couldn't wiggle his fingers at all," said Ollie. "That must mean that your arm isn't broken. I guess that's a good thing, isn't it?"

Relieved, Fae lowered her arm. "It is," she agreed.

To her surprise, Ollie sat down in the grass right beside her as if they were old friends. "Did you just move here?" he asked.

"No. I've been here since June," Fae told him.

"But that's almost two months. How come you never come out to play? I've never even seen you before."

"Grandma says I have to hide," said Fae. "Actually, I'm not supposed to be talking to you. Nobody's allowed to know about me."

"Really? Why not?" asked Ollie. "Is there something wrong with you?"

The words sent a cold jolt down Fae's spine. She knew there was something wrong with her, but she had no idea what, and she wished she knew so that she could change it and make herself right again. Even Mama couldn't tell her what it was that was wrong, no matter how many times Fae had asked her.

The last time Fae had asked Mama what was wrong with her was at the train station. Not the pleasant little one out in the country where she'd first met Grandma and Grandpa, but the big, loud, smoky, noisy place in the town. It was scary there, and there were strangers pushing and shoving and shouting at each other everywhere. Fae clung tightly to Mama's dress as the crowd surged around them. Some of the men shouted rude things at Mama or tried to touch her, but she flinched out of the way and managed to get herself and Fae all the way up to the platform.

"There," said Mama, once they were facing the open doors of the train. Looking up at her, Fae saw she had dark circles underneath her eyes and her hair was straggly and messy. She pushed some of it back behind her ear and looked down at Fae. Her smile was faded, like an old dress that had been washed too many times and didn't have much use left in it.

"We made it safely here." She knelt down and brushed the dust from Fae's shoes, smoothed down her hair, did up the top button of her little frock. "Now you have to be a good girl for me, Fae."

"Are Grandma and Grandpa nice, Mama?" Fae whispered.

Mama hesitated. "They're nicer than he is," she said, at last. "You'll be happy there." Tears shone in her eyes as she pulled a handkerchief out from her sleeve. "You'll have a good life there, Fae, a better life than I can give you here in London. You'll have a chance. The same chance that I did." She sighed. "I just hope you grow up into someone who doesn't throw it away like I did."

Fae didn't know what Mama was talking about. "But I don't want a life there," she said, pleadingly. "I want to stay here with you."

"Oh, Fae. I told you. You can't," said Mama, her voice breaking a little.

"But why not?" Fae begged. "What's wrong with me? What did I do wrong? Why can't I stay?"

"Oh, my darling." The tears spilled out of Mama's eyes. She leaned closer and wrapped her arms tightly around Fae, pulling her close to her chest. "You did nothing wrong. Nothing at all. There's nothing wrong with you."

"Then why are you sending me away, Mama? What did I do?"

Mama drew back, wiping her eyes as she straightened up. "It's not about your mistakes, Fae," she whispered. "It's about mine."

Fae wanted to ask what Mama meant. Then there was a shrill whistle, and a man appeared on the platform beside Fae, dressed in a smart uniform.

"All aboard!" he shouted.

"Mama..." Fae whimpered.

"Go." Mama wiped her eyes quickly. "Go, Fae."

"But..." Fae started forward.

The man in the uniform grabbed her arm. "Come on, little one," he said. "You don't want to miss your train, do you?"

Fae did want to miss her train. She wanted to miss it more than anything else in the world. "Mama!" she shrieked. "Mama! Come back!"

But Mama was backing away into the crowd, and the conductor was dragging her toward the train, and Fae still didn't know what it was that was wrong with her. What was so wrong with her that the man hated her?

What was so wrong with her that Mama sent her away?

"Well?" Ollie prompted, snapping Fae out of her thoughts. "What's wrong with you? Are you sick?"

"I'm not sick," said Fae. "I – I don't know what's wrong with me."

"That's rather odd," said Ollie. He grinned. "Maybe your parents have to hide you away like pirates hide buried treasure. To keep you safe."

Fae had never thought about it like that before, but the boy's grin made her want to believe it.

"I don't have parents," she told him. "Just a mama, but she's not here. I live with my grandma and grandpa."

"That's what I figured," said Ollie. "My parents are friends with them. Your grandma is scary."

Fae laughed. "She's very scary," she said. "So why aren't you in church?"

"I was sick this morning. I threw up on my shoes," said Ollie. "Mama said I should stay home, but I feel better now, so I came out to play." He glanced up at the sun. "They'll probably be home soon. I'd better go."

"Wait." Fae grabbed Ollie's arm. "Don't go yet."

"Sorry," said Ollie regretfully, backing away. "Mama will skin me alive if she sees I went outside."

"And my grandma will kill me if she knows you saw me," said Fae urgently. "Ollie, please don't tell anyone about me. I – I have to be a secret."

Ollie grinned. "I'm good at keeping secrets," he said.

And when he scampered off, Fae felt like his words were precious little jewels she could carry around deep in her heart. Something that glowed in the dark, no matter how lonely she would become.

CHAPTER 3

Four Years Later

"Hurry up with those, girl!" snapped Grandma. "What's taking so long?"

"I'll be right there, Grandma!" called Fae. She knelt in front of the oven, carefully grasping the baking tray. She lifted it up onto the top of the stove. The scones had come out well, she was relieved to see. If they didn't, sometimes Grandma would hit her with her cane.

"Smells good," said Grandpa, taking a deep breath. The breath ended in a spasm of coughs that shook his emaciated frame, making him tremble in his chair.

"Don't talk so much, Reginald," snapped Grandma. "It's bad

for your health. What are you doing over there, Fae? Where are those scones?"

"Right here, Grandma," said Fae. She slipped two scones onto a plate and brought them to the table. Moving quickly to avoid Grandma's wrath, she sliced them neatly and began to butter them. Their mouthwatering scent filled the whole room, but Fae knew she wouldn't get to taste them until after her grandparents had eaten.

"Thank you, love," murmured Grandpa as Fae put his scone down in front of him.

"Hmph. Why are these so small?" demanded Grandma, glaring down at her scone. "Can't you even bake scones properly, girl?" She shook her head grumpily. "Considering what your mother was, I suppose I should be surprised you can bake at all."

Her words still stung, even though four long years had passed since Fae had come to live with her grandparents. Four years in which she hadn't heard a single word from her mama, even though Mama had promised so many times to write. Fae had composed a few letters to Mama, but every time she tried to get Grandma to post them for her, Grandma had angrily ripped them up and thrown them into the fire. Sometimes it felt like Mama had been nothing but a blurry dream.

She cleared away the table once her grandparents had eaten, keeping her head down and trying not to let them see how much Grandma's words had upset her. Taking the plates back into the scullery, she filled the sink with water from a bucket that Grandpa had drawn from the well earlier that morning. As she started piling the dishes into the sink, she grabbed a dry scone from the baking tray and took a hungry bite. It was fluffy and buttery and almost still warm.

"Fae!" shouted Grandma.

Swallowing so quickly she nearly choked, Fae hurried back into the kitchen. "Yes, Grandma?"

"Your grandfather and I are going to the market." Grandma was pulling her coat around her shoulders, giving Fae a glare over the top of her hook nose. "As usual, we have to get groceries – you're eating us out of house and home. Why I ever agreed to another mouth to feed, heaven only knows." She pulled on her bonnet and tied it with jerky little movements. "Stay here and behave yourself."

"Yes, Grandma," said Fae, hanging her head.

Grandma stepped out the door, and Grandpa paused beside Fae, putting his big knotty hand on top of her head. "Everyone's going to the Christmas market today," he whispered to her, giving her a tiny wink. "I think it's safe for you to play outside, if you're careful."

"Really?" Fae grinned up at him.

"Shhh!" Grandpa glanced up at Grandma's back; she was already heading out to their cart. "Really," he added quietly, touching Fae's cheek with the back of his forefinger. "Be a good girl, now."

"Yes, Grandpa."

She waited just long enough for him to close the door behind him before she raced out into the back garden, leaving the sink full of dishes abandoned and forgotten. The winter morning was still and crisp and white, the lawn as perfect as newly starched sheets; the great tree's bare branches were twisted in a black silhouette against the sky. Fae's feet crunched in the snow as she ran up to the trunk of the tree and laid her hands on its rough bark. The seasons had been spinning around this tree for so long, yet the tree was always the same, and its presence lent to Fae the constant warmth of an old friendship.

"Hello, tree," she told it. "I get to play here with you this morning."

"Pssst!"

Fae looked up. Two sparkling eyes, hiding in the hedge bordering the garden on one side, looked back at her.

"Ollie!" Fae cried, laughing as she ran toward him.

Ollie tumbled out of the hedge. "Catch me if you can!" he shouted.

Giggling uncontrollably, Fae ran toward him. Ollie ducked and dodged, his legs much longer than hers, but she was only a few steps behind; then feinting left, then plunging right, Fae was always in his wake, her arms outstretched to him, shrieking with delight. The sun smiled down on them, the sky was bluer just because of their laughter; snow sprayed and crackled under their feet as if to cheer them on. It felt as though the whole world was spinning around just this moment, and then the whole world was just spinning of its own accord as they both fell dizzily to the snow beneath the tree and lay on their backs, giggling at how beautiful the day was and how wonderful it was to be young.

"How did you know I'd be outside today?" Fae panted, looking over at Ollie.

There were snowflakes tangled up in his brown hair, and his face was red. "I thought your grandparents might be going to the market, so I got my parents to leave me at home and take my brothers there instead," he said. "I hate the market anyway – there's too many people, and it's so noisy and all we do is carry wreaths up and down all day. I'd far rather be at home, reading, and I know I get in the way. Mama was happy to leave me here."

"What are you reading about?" asked Fae.

"It's called *The Life and Adventures of Robinson Crusoe*," said Ollie. "It's all about a man who gets stuck on an island all by himself. He has to do all kinds of things to stay alive. It's very exciting."

"I don't think it would be exciting to be stuck somewhere

without anyone else," said Fae. "It's not very exciting to be stuck in a house all by yourself."

"It must be so boring." Ollie flipped over onto his stomach, propping his chin up in his hands.

"It's better now that you're teaching me how to read," said Fae, smiling.

"Reading is wonderful," said Ollie. "My brothers don't think so, though. They always tease me about it because I just want to read instead of playing knights or soldiers or pirates with them." He pushed his spectacles a little further up on the bridge of his nose. "I think reading is much more interesting than hitting each other and wrestling."

"I think you're interesting," said Fae, giggling.

"Interesting!" Ollie laughed. "And I think you're fascinating, so there."

They lay back in the sunshine, staring up at the dappled light through the branches of the old tree, telling each other stories about the objects and animals they could make out in the shapes of the twigs and light, and Fae didn't say what she really thought Ollie was.

She thought he was the sunshine in a dark room.

Fae pushed the mop back into the bucket, swirling it

around and watching the soapy water turn a deeper brown. Slopping water back onto the kitchen floor and working the mop across the stone, she glanced up at the cuckoo clock on top of the kitchen cupboard. It was past one in the afternoon already, and there was still no sign of Grandma and Grandpa. Ollie had gone home for lunch. Where could they be?

Sometimes Mama would leave her alone in their house, too, when she was little. She never left Edith, though – just like she never sent Edith away. Fae wondered how her little sister was doing. She would be walking already, of course. Jabbering away, too. It hurt Fae's heart to wonder whether Edith would ever be able to say the name *Fae*. She had wished so hard for that day to come when she was little and playing with her baby sister.

"Say, 'Fae', Edith," she'd said, over and over. Was there anyone left who would teach Edith to say the name? Did Edith even remember her?

Hooves clattered outside, and Fae hurried to put the mop back into the bucket and put them both in the scullery. As she trotted toward the front door, though, she realized that the sound was not the slow clip-clop of old George the donkey bringing the cart back from the market. This was the sound of several hooves – a fast carriage. Nerves gripped Fae's gut. Nobody ever came here when Grandma and Grandpa weren't at home. What was going on?

She opened the door just a crack, peering out into the farmyard. Two big, strong horses had just come to a halt, bits of snow still swirling around their legs, drawing a carriage – Fae had seen it before sometimes; one of Grandma's friends always came to tea parties in it. A pale young widow, Mrs. Willows, was climbing out of the carriage right now, fanning herself as she twittered to her two footmen. They followed, and between them, they carried the limp form of Fae's grandmother.

"Oh no!" Fae couldn't help but shout out in panic. The door swung open, and Mrs. Willows startled visibly, staring at her.

"What happened?" Fae cried.

Grandpa stumbled out of the wagon close behind the footmen who were carrying Grandma. He hurried ahead, pulling the door open.

"Go and get her bed ready for her, Fae," he told her. His voice was quick and shaky, different from its usual slow kindness, and it frightened her.

"Who on Earth is this little urchin?" demanded Mrs. Willows.

Grandpa didn't reply. "Go, Fae," he ordered.

Fae ran up the stairs two at a time, heading to Grandma and Grandpa's bedroom. She had already made the bed earlier that morning, but now she quickly closed the window to keep the wintry air out, plumping up Grandma's pillows exactly the way she liked them. There were footsteps on the stairs, and

Grandpa stumbled in, holding the door for the footmen with Grandma.

"Have you no smelling salts?" asked Mrs. Willows as the footmen laid Grandma on the bed. She pulled off Grandma's shoes and began to rub her feet.

"I... I don't know," murmured Grandpa, staring down at his unconscious wife.

"We do." Fae pulled open a drawer in the big old wardrobe and held out the smelling salts to Mrs. Willows, who gave her a repulsed glance before grabbing the salts and holding them under Grandma's nose.

To Fae's relief, Grandma's eyes fluttered. In a moment, the old lady sat up, her eyes flashing as she glared around the room.

"What are you doing in my house?" she shrieked at the footmen, but her voice sounded different – weak and wobbly and wet. She coughed, the sound like rocks grinding in her chest.

"Go," said Mrs. Willows, pointing at the footmen. They hurried out. "How are you feeling now, my dear Theodora?" she asked.

"Oh, simply terrible, my dear," said Grandma, leaning back against her pillows. Fae believed her. Her face was red and flushed, gleaming with sweat; Fae had never seen her grandmother sweat before. "This is the end of me, I'm sure. It must be that influenza that's been going around the village. Reginald has had it for days – and now he's given it to me."

"Now, now, Dora, dear." Grandpa shuffled closer and smiled at Grandma. "It'll be all right."

Fae climbed up onto the bed. She knew she wasn't allowed to, but she just couldn't help it. She reached for Grandma's hand.

"What's wrong, Grandma?" she asked. "Are you sick?"

"Grandma?" Mrs. Willows stared at Fae. "Theodora, who is this?"

"Oh, mind your own business, Ethel," snapped Grandma.

Mrs. Willows stepped back, staring in confusion at Fae. "But she called you her grandmother."

"I told you to mind your own business!" Grandma's voice rose to a screech. "Get out of my house!"

Confused, Mrs. Willows gave Fae one last frightened glance and then ran outside. The shouting seemed to have exhausted Grandma. She lay back on her pillows, panting, and Grandpa sat down slowly in his armchair beside the bed. He reached out and intertwined his fingers with Grandma's.

"You'll be all right, Dora," he murmured.

"I'm not well, Reginald." Grandma's voice was weak and, for the first time since Fae could remember, frightened. "I'm not well at all."

"I'll go for the doctor soon, dear," said Grandpa. Fae could see the sweat glittering on his own forehead. His hand was trembling where he held Grandma's; Fae wasn't sure if it was from fear or weakness. "I just need to catch my breath."

"Is Grandma sick, Grandpa?" Fae whispered.

"Yes, my dear." Grandpa looked up at her, his rheumy eyes bright with fever. "We are both sick. You'll need to help us now, do you understand? You need to help us."

"I'll help you, Grandpa," whimpered Fae. "I promise I'll help you."

"You're a good girl, Fae." Grandpa leaned back in his chair, his eyes closing as he drifted to sleep. "You're a good girl."

But standing in the room with her grandparents as they both slowly fell asleep, Fae didn't feel like she could do anything to help them. She didn't know what to do. And she didn't feel like a good girl – or, at least, a good enough girl – at all.

TWILIGHT WAS FALLING SLOWLY OVER THE COUNTRYSIDE, a familiar sight to Fae from her perch in the old oak tree. That precious hour somewhere between day and night was Fae's last chance of the day to see the outside world, to climb as high as she could into the tree's forgiving boughs and gaze out at the wide world she was never allowed to go out into. But this time, she had climbed higher than ever before. She clung to one of the topmost branches of the tree, feeling it sway gently every time that she shifted her weight, her eyes searching every field and road in the fading light. Yet there was no sign of Ollie.

He was the only person that Fae could think of who could help her and her grandparents. In fact, he was the only person Fae knew aside from her grandparents, and she knew that they were both equally sick. Neither of them had risen from their places since they got home, and every now and then one of them would start coughing – dark, hard, heavy coughs that sounded like they could hardly breathe. Fae could almost feel them slipping away before her very eyes. She didn't know what to do. She couldn't think of a way to help them. But Ollie could help them, and Fae sat in the tree waiting for him, praying that he would come out.

Ollie didn't come out. Fae didn't know why; normally he would at least come by to say hello in the evenings. When complete darkness fell and there was still no sign of him, she was crushed by disappointment.

"Fae!" Grandma's faint voice still managed to be harsh from inside the house. "Come..." The rest of her sentence was lost in coughing.

Shivering in the cold, Fae shimmied down the tree and left a lonely set of tracks across the white lawn as she headed back into the house. She paused to put on a pot of tea, hoping it would do something, and climbed the stairs to her grandparents' room.

She could hear them talking as she approached. "... very ill," her grandfather was saying. "You need to see a doctor, Dora. If not, then..." He paused. "It might not be good."

"Go for the doctor, then, Reginald."

"Oh, my love, I would, and I want to, but I fear it would do no good. I'm just as unable to get up from this chair as you are to rise from your bed. We are sick, my darling, very sick."

"Then what do you propose we do? Die here alone?" Grandma demanded.

"We can send Fae. She's a little thing, but she's brave. If she knew why we were sending her, she would find her way to the doctor's, or at least to the neighbors', and send for help."

"No. Absolutely not. That child cannot be seen. I will not have it," said Grandma.

"Dora, please. Try to be reasonable," pleaded Grandpa. "Your life depends on it."

"I would rather die than let my shame be known," snapped Grandma. "The child stays here, Reginald. And if that's how you feel, then so do we."

Fae knew that they were talking about her, and she knew it was her fault that they were both sick. Tears filling her eyes, she slunk quietly back down to the kitchen to wait for the teapot to boil. She had to save them somehow. She had to; otherwise, their deaths would be all her fault.

CHAPTER 4

Fae must have fallen asleep somewhere in between pleading Grandma to eat her soup and gently sponging her blazing forehead with cool water, because when she awoke with a start, she was still clutching the cold, dry cloth in her hand. She looked around the room, searching for the terrible, crackling noise that had woken her. It took her a moment to realize that it was coming from Grandma.

"Grandma?" Fae raised herself from the pillows on Grandpa's side of the bed and grabbed Grandma's hand. Her fingers were clenched into a tight fist, her eyes staring, her mouth wide as she sucked in another struggling breath. It sounded like she was drowning even where she lay; the sheets were sodden with her sweat.

"Grandma, what's the matter?" Fae gasped, staring down at her. "Say something. Please, Grandma, say something!"

Grandma's eyes rolled to meet Fae's, and what she saw in them was pure, naked terror. Her fist opened just a little, just enough for Fae to slip her hand inside and feel her fingers being clenched in a death grip. Grandma's lips worked, struggling around her rattling breaths, as she tried to form a word. But Fae couldn't hear. She clung to Grandma's hand, leaning closer.

"What are you saying, Grandma?"

"Reg... Reg..." Grandma tried. Her thin chest heaved with effort and she squirmed as if something was hurting or pinching her.

"What is it? What do you want?" Fae begged. She felt a hot tear run down her cheek as she stared at Grandma's pale face. Her lips were blue, her eyes popping, and Fae could hear the terrible tread of approaching death. She could feel its presence in her bones.

"Grandma, please." Fae was clinging to Grandma's hand as tightly as she could.

Grandma's eyes rolled back in her head. She took a great gasp, gurgling in her failing lungs, and finally managed to speak. It was just one word.

"Reginald," she whispered.

With the word, the struggle seemed to leave her. Her gasping breaths stopped; her shaking chest stilled. In Fae's hand, her fingers went limp, and she seemed to sag within herself. As if something more than breath had left her body and fled, flung through the bedroom window, fleeing out into the starry skies of a perfect winter night.

"Grandma?" Fae stared into Grandma's eyes, but Grandma did not stare back. Her eyes were no longer cold or sharp or vindictive; they were just objects, glazed and glassy. "No." Fae's throat closed. "No, no, no. Grandma. Grandma, wake up!" She seized her grandmother's shoulders, screaming now. "Grandma, you have to wake up! Come on, Grandma. You've got to wake up. Wake up!" Desperate, eliciting no response from Grandma's limp body, she turned to the armchair where Grandpa was still sitting. "Grandpa, please, you have to help her!" she begged. "Do something. Please, Grandpa, do something."

Grandpa was sitting still, his chin on his chest, asleep. Fae couldn't believe her screams hadn't woken him. Desperate with fear, she scrambled over Grandma's body and reached out to grab his arm. "Grandpa!"

But something was wrong. She knew it the moment she touched his flesh. It was cold. So cold – cold as the air around her, cold as the terror forming right now in her heart.

"Grandpa?"

She was breathless, the word barely a whisper. Goosebumps

rose on her skin as she gave him a gentle shake. He lolled limply in the chair, and that was when Fae knew that her grandfather was dead, too. He had died the way he had lived – quietly, without a fuss, and in Grandma's shadow.

"No!" The cry that ripped itself loose from Fae's throat was less of a word than the howl of a wounded animal. She heard it reverberate around the house, shaking the windowpanes like a physical manifestation of the black, cold feeling that had seized her heart.

"Nooooooo! Grandma! Grandpa!"

There was no response from either of them, and Fae knew that she was sitting in a room with two dead bodies, two cold still dead bodies and Grandma's eyes were turning misty and strange. Panic seized her. There was only one thing Fae could think of to do: she had to hide. Crashing out of the room, she bolted down the stairs, half-falling and half-running, stumbling into the kitchen. She yanked open the nearest cupboard and climbed inside, wedging her body in between the flour sack and the wall. There in the dark, no one could get her. There in the dark, she was alone and safe.

Except something had followed her in there: her thoughts. They were dark and boiling, tumbling in her head, a bubbling stew of broken-heartedness, and the ugliest ingredient of it all floated to the top. A thought that made her tremble.

Grandma didn't get the doctor because she didn't want him to know about Fae. And if she had gotten the doctor, then maybe she and Grandpa would still be alive today.

Fae managed to breathe just three words before the sobs overtook her.

"I killed them."

※

IT FELT AS THOUGH FAE'S LIMBS HAD FUSED TO THE BRANCH of the great tree. She had never been so cold in her life; it felt as though her heart, soul, and body were as gray and frigid as the dawn that was just breaking miserably over the eastern horizon. She huddled against the branch, lying on it with her arms and legs wrapped around the bark, clinging to it as if it was an old friend. Perhaps if she stayed her long enough and if it got cold enough, she would freeze to the tree, assimilate into it somehow. Maybe her roots would grow down into the rich earth and anchor her deeply there, and she would able to grow tall too, to stand for centuries unchanged by the puny human tragedies that took place beneath her mighty boughs. To feel nothing except the breeze in her branches.

But Fae didn't turn into an unfeeling tree, no matter how hard she tried. As the morning broke and warmth began to seep back into her bones, she kept gazing toward the common, feeling as though she had been ripped open inside somehow. It was only her desperate need to find help that had driven her out of her hiding place in the kitchen cupboard sometime deep in the night, and she knew exactly who would be able to help her.

Ollie.

She just had to wait here on the branch. Sooner or later, he would come along with a book under his arm, whistling and pretending not to be glancing around for her behind his thick round spectacles. The other boys would run into the common and start shouting and running about, and he would come toward her and call her name softly, and she'd run to him and tell him everything. Everything would be all right if Ollie came.

The day warmed up still more, and Fae lay listless on the branch as the pattern of shadows changed around her. The sun walked slowly up the long hill of the morning and reached its summit, and still the lanes remained empty. Not even an ox cart or a laden donkey came past, not a beggar or a single child. And definitely not Ollie. As the day began to slip away into afternoon, Fae sat up at last, her heart hollow with the knowledge that nobody was going to come. Nor could she go looking for anyone; then they would all know she had killed her grandparents.

When dusk fell and the cold began to nip at her toes and fingers again, Fae sat up, slowly loosening her stiff joints from their hold on the tree. She had never climbed down at such a glacial pace in her life. It was up to her now. Her thoughts felt sluggish, half-frozen by grief. Dead people were buried, weren't they? In the ground. She'd have to try. She couldn't just leave them there. Opening the door of the dusty garden shed, she shuddered as rats scuttled into the darkness. She could see the big shovel leaning against the back wall, but to get there she'd have to traverse a dark mess of broken pottery and cobwebs. Instead, she reached for a little trowel near the door and wandered back out into the garden.

Scraping the snow aside with her foot, Fae uncovered the dark earth. Kneeling, she took the trowel and dug it determinedly into the ground – or at least, she tried. Only the tip of the trowel went in, making a soft noise like *chink* as it met the iced soil. Choking back a sob, Fae tried to scoop the dirt away, but all she managed to do was scratch the surface of the earth.

Tears were gushing down her cheeks as she ran back into the house. She wished she could scream for help, but instead, she just ran into the bedroom where her grandparents were still lying, their bodies exactly as they had been last night. Untouched. Abandoned.

"Grandpa, I'm so sorry." Fae sank to the floor at the feet of the chair, leaning her forehead against his legs. He was still wearing his old house slippers. "I'm so sorry. I don't know what to do. I didn't mean to do it. I'm so sorry."

There was no reply. There never would be.

THE ROOM WAS FILLED WITH PALE LIGHT WHEN FAE AWOKE. She sat up slowly, raising a hand to her cheek, which felt bruised and reddened from the pressure on the cold planks of the wooden floor. She was so cold. Looking up, the first thing that she saw was Grandpa's face, and she was shocked by the way it looked in the brutal morning light. There was no color in it anymore; his eyes were closed, his jaw slack, mouth open so that she could see his old yellow teeth. The naked sunlight made his face look leathery somehow. Like he was some kind of a puppet. As if everything that made him Grandpa – his smile, his gentle voice, the look in his eyes when Fae knew he was sorry for Grandma's harsh words, the way he tapped out his pipe, his deep love for jam tarts – was just gone. It wasn't there and dead; it was gone, somewhere else, as surely as a room was emptier when there was no one in it.

It was in that moment that Fae realized they were gone, irretrievably gone, and there was nothing more she could do. The choking grief of yesterday was replaced by a kind of hollowness. She suddenly realized how hungry she was, and that there was no one to go to the market and buy eggs for breakfast anymore, or to tend the sheep and old George.

Slowly, she got up and went over to the linen cupboard. Pulling two clean sheets out of the highest drawer she could reach, she went over to the two empty bodies and spread the sheets over them. Moving mechanically, she went to her little room and gathered up her spare dress, her coat, her shoes, and her dolly. She stuffed them into Grandma's least favorite bag, added the food she could find in the house, and hoisted the bag onto the shoulders. Then, pausing only to open the stable door so that George could go out into the pasture, she headed out of the house and began to walk down the lane.

There was only one person she could think of that could help her now. Mama.

PART II

CHAPTER 5

The railway was the only thing that Fae could think of that connected the world of her grandparents and their blazing countryside with the city of her memories. From Grandma and Grandpa's talking, she knew at least that the city had a name: London. She also knew the train had brought her to the country, and the train ran along a long, straight track, much faster than she could walk. But at least she *could* walk, and she knew which direction to take.

The streets were still completely empty. Fae saw that all of the houses had wreaths on the doorways and there were candles in every window; she had heard Ollie talk about Christmas before, but Grandma never allowed it to come into their house, saying that Fae didn't deserve to have Christmas. Ollie had talked about candles in the window at Christmas. Ollie had also not come to her when she needed it, and the thought was almost worse than the memory of her two dead grandparents alone and abandoned in their bedroom.

She tried not to think about it. Instead, she reached the train station, more or less only because the entire village was built around it. She remembered that the train had been facing toward the church when she'd first gotten here four years ago, so she would have to go the opposite way, toward the desolate white fields. Pausing to take an apple out of her bag, she headed along the tracks, stepping from one board to the other as she gnawed on the apple. It tasted like sawdust.

She wondered how long it would take to get to London. It had taken her a few hours by train. Would it take half a day on foot? A whole day? What would she do when it started to get dark? She didn't know, but as the day wore on, her feet grew more and more painful, and the air grew more and more chilly.

Fae hadn't known the world was so big. Every time she thought London would be just over the next hill, she would reach the top only to see there was another hill directly ahead, and then another, and another. She passed through a small town, but carefully, darting from one hiding place to the next so nobody noticed her. That was somewhere in the late afternoon; by dusk, she knew her feet were blistered and bleeding, and it had begun to snow, and she couldn't see to the top of the next hill. All she could see was the next sleeper in front of her, and the next, and the next. She knew she couldn't stop. To stop would be to freeze. So, she just kept stepping as snow settled on her shoulders and the night turned pitch black around her.

After a while, it began to feel as though Fae were the only person in the world, like everything else had simply melted into the fog and vanished. She thought maybe she'd become trapped in a snow globe, a tiny china figure of a little girl walking along a railway, as if the night would never end, as if there was nobody left in the whole universe. It would have been terrible, if she hadn't just seen her grandparents die. Nothing could be more terrible than that.

Her legs were starting to wobble under her when she heard the steady clop-clop of a horse's hooves. Pausing on the tracks, she looked behind her. A light was heading toward her, haloed in the fog; she could make out the corner of a wooden cart, painted bright yellow. Not knowing what else to do, Fae just turned and kept walking.

The cart drew nearer. In a minute, she could see the steam rising from the horse's back. It was patched black and white like a cow in the lantern light, and its driver was swarthy and a little scary – Fae had seen people like him camp on the common grounds. Gypsies, Grandma had called them, and refused to let Fae go outside. She said they stole children and ate them.

"Hello," the driver called. "Where are you headed?"

Fae stopped and looked up at him. She was too tired to be scared. "Are you going to eat me?" she asked.

"Eat you? No thank you, dear," said the driver. He gave her a gap-toothed grin, and Fae saw that his brown eyes were kind. "I just had a little girl in the last town – I'm quite full."

Fae stared at him.

"I'm joking, lass," said the driver. "I don't eat girls, or people of any gender, for that matter. I'm just an old tinker." He sat back against his yellow cart and studied her with gentle eyes. "So, where are you going?"

"London," said Fae.

"I'm going in that direction." The gypsy patted the driver's seat. "Would you like to ride along? Old Samson doesn't mind another weight, do you, Samson?" he asked, addressing the horse.

The horse whinnied.

"Samson doesn't mind," said the tinker. "In fact, he says you're more than welcome. He'd like some more sophisticated company than a silly old tinker."

Fae couldn't help but smile at his manner. She took a tentative step nearer. "Are you sure you don't eat people?"

"Quite sure, last time I checked," said the tinker with a wink.

Fae's feet were so tired, and she didn't know if she'd ever get to London on foot. Maybe there was some kind of magic that meant only carts or trains could get there. Mutely, she shuffled over to the cart. The tinker shifted up to make room, and she climbed up beside him, feeling a wave of relief as she took the weight off her feet at last.

"There you go," said the tinker, smiling. "London, you say?"

"London," said Fae.

The tinker didn't ask any more questions. He just cracked the whip and the cart rocked on into the darkness.

"Time to wake up, dear. I can't go no further than this."

The sun was warm on Fae's back. As she sat up slowly, something began to slide off her; she grabbed for it instinctively, and her fingers met warm fur. It was the tinker's coat. It smelt faintly of pipe tobacco, a scent that reminded Fae of Grandpa and made her heart hurt for home.

She blinked, rubbing her eyes with her free hand as she clutched the coat in her lap. The day was warm and bright, and every snowbank seemed to be glittering with sun, as if thousands of tiny diamonds had been strewn across the landscape. The cart was stopped on the verge of a crossroads and Samson was resting patiently in the shafts, his blinkered head held low as he dozed.

Fae looked up at the tinker. "Is this London?" she asked sleepily.

"Not yet, not quite," said the tinker. "My road's taking me another way. But we're closer – much closer than we were last night, in any case." He smiled. "You slept sound as a baby. You sure you don't have gypsy blood? A moving cart is a rocking crib to a gypsy."

Fae shrugged. "I don't know what blood I have," she said. "I don't have a papa."

"You must have a papa, dear," said the tinker kindly.

Fae shrugged again. The tinker seemed content with that. He reached into a pocket in the front of his waistcoat and pulled out something that sparkled like the snow. "Here," he said.

Fae held out her hands, and he dropped it into her palm. She peered at the small, hard shape. It was a crystal on a piece of string, glittering in the sun, as if warm light could turn pale crystal into a thousand shimmering colors.

"It's so pretty," said Fae, with a gasp.

"It was given to me by a young woman in London." The tinker sighed, his eyes turning wistful. "You remind me of her. I'll never see her again, so it seems fitting for you to have it."

Fae slipped the string over her head. The crystal lay against her chest, close as an old friend. "Thank you," she whispered. "You've been very kind."

"When you look at it, little one…" The tinker paused, biting his lip. "Just never be afraid to shine, all right?"

Fae clambered down from the cart. "Which way is London?" she asked.

"That way." The tinker pointed with his whip. "Keep going for an hour or two and you'll find a small town. They have a busy market today, and many of the carts belong to merchants who'll move on to London next to sell their wares. Find a cart and hide under its canvas. With any luck, you'll be in London by nightfall."

"Thank you," said Fae, smiling at the tinker. She clutched the crystal. "You've been so good to me."

His expression softened. "I hope you find whatever you're looking for, little one." He snapped the whip. "Come on, Samson! Let's go."

Fae turned and started heading down the road the tinker had indicated so that she didn't have to watch him go. She felt curiously as though she'd lost something when she heard the cart's rumbling recede into the distance, although she couldn't put her finger on why. Something about the tinker had been strangely familiar.

She tried to forget about him as she moved forward with a new sense of purpose. She had a plan now, and she took out the last chunk of bread she'd managed to bring with her and nibbled it as she moved briskly along the road. By the time the bread was done, she could see the town the tinker had been talking about. It lay at the bottom of a little valley, hugged by the surrounding hills; she had the feeling that it was normally as peaceful as the town where she'd lived until recently, but not today.

As Fae moved closer, hiding in the shadows of trees and hedges, she could hear loud shouting coming from the marketplace at the center of the village. People were peddling their wares, haggling over prices, singing drunken songs; somewhere an auction was happening, and the auctioneer was almost drowned out by the magnificent chaos of the market day.

Fae hid in a nook between two empty carts and peered out into the marketplace. It was a mass of movement, noise and color unlike anything she'd ever seen before. Stallholders were standing with their wares in their hands, shouting out bargains: "Two for a shilling! Tuppence for four!" Women strolled among the food stalls, their children clinging to their skirts. They bought something here and there, slowly filling the baskets they carried on their arms.

Some of the shoppers, however, were men. These carried large pouches of money and were followed by burly men who never said anything, and they bought things by the crate. Then the burly men would pick up the crates and disappear out of the marketplace.

Fae slipped across the busy marketplace, her heart pounding with fear, but nobody noticed her, and soon she was safely tucked away behind some barrels of fish next to one of the vendors. She watched, hiding behind the furthest barrel from the shoppers, as one of the rich men – merchants, Fae guessed – stepped up to the vendor. They haggled for a moment, and then the vendor spat in his hand and held it out. The merchant followed suit, and they shook.

Two men, their shoulders rippling like living boulders under their shirts, picked up one of the barrels and started to head off. Fae hurried after them, slipping from shadow to shadow to stay hidden. They went out of the marketplace and into a square beyond where rows of carts were waiting, harnessed to donkeys, mules, oxen and horses. It was to a horse cart that the two men took the barrel. They lifted it up into the cart and tugged the canvas cover over it.

"Finally, he's done," said one of the men, climbing up into the driver's seat. "How can it take so long of a Saturday morning to buy a week's provisions for one small tavern?"

"Hush, Crowther," snapped his companion. "He'll be out any minute and in a hurry to get back to London. Don't let him hear you."

As they spoke, Fae scampered scarily close until she reached the cart where the two men were sitting. Holding her breath, she crawled underneath it and cowered under its belly for a moment. The two men kept bickering, oblivious to her presence. With a rush of relief, Fae crawled to the back of the cart, lifted the canvas and climbed underneath. She let the canvas slip back down again and found herself a hiding place between the fish barrel and a large crate of vegetables.

A moment later, a third voice joined in the conversation, and there was the sound of a cracking whip. The cart lurched forward, Fae grabbing at the crate to keep her balance. She felt it bump over cobblestones, the horses turning this way and that, and finally they seemed to settle into a rhythm and Fae could feel that they were on the open road.

A pulse of excitement shot through her veins. They were on their way to London. She was heading toward Mama at last.

She opened her food bag and looked inside, feeling a rush of disappointment as she saw that she'd finished it all. Laying the bag back down, she stared longingly at the crate beside her. Under the tarp, there was the shadow of a fat, orange carrot right on the top of it, looking so juicy that she could almost taste its crisp sweetness on her tongue. She reached toward it, then drew her hand back. What would Grandma say if Fae stole something? She complained enough if Fae even looked at a piece of food without asking. Would she be angry?

Then she remembered that Grandma wasn't here to be angry. The realization took the last of her strength from her. She leaned back against the barrel, took the carrot, and started chewing on the end of it. And she wasn't sure if she was heartbroken or liberated.

CHAPTER 6

Fae was being rocked. She almost wanted to tell Mama that she was too big to be rocked in a crib now; she was ten years old already, after all. But the feeling was so deliciously soothing. She wished Mama had given her a mattress and a pillow for the crib, though. The hard wooden boards were digging into her spine, and her neck was crooked uncomfortably against the back. In fact, her whole body felt stiff and tender from being rocked in this bare crib. As she squirmed, trying to get comfortable, the crib began to jolt instead of rocking. It shook and bumped, and Fae was uncomfortable. She wanted Mama to stop. She wanted to get up…

"Hey!" shouted a harsh, male voice. "Get out of the way! I'll run you over, you little street rat!"

Fae sat up with a gasp of alarm. It was almost completely

dark. She blinked, flailing a little as there was another heavy bump, completely disoriented. She wasn't safe in her crib – she was in some dark, dusty place, and there were unfamiliar voices all around her, and... vegetables?

She was still in the cart. Fae struggled to wake herself, pulling her bag sleepily toward her. She must have fallen asleep somewhere along the road to London.

Now, they had come to a halt. She heard the driver's voice. "We're here at last. Let's get this all offloaded so that we can get to the Lame Horse."

"Sounds good to me," said the other man.

Fae clasped the cloth of her bag in her teeth and crawled to the back of the cart. She nosed her way out of the canvas, dropped silently to the cobblestones, and ran to the nearest dark space she could see – an alleyway so narrow that it could barely contain a few broken old barrels and Fae's skinny form hidden in between them. She waited until the cart was offloaded and driven away before stepping out from her hiding place and walking slowly down the street.

She had forgotten just how busy London was; how much noise there was. How many people. As she walked out of the street and into a market square – it looked familiar; it had to look familiar, she had lived somewhere nearby, she must have... She realized that there were probably more people gathered in that one square than there had been in the entire town back home. No. She couldn't think of the countryside, of her grandparents' house, as home anymore. Home had been somewhere they were, and they weren't anymore. Home was with Mama now.

Mama. Fae stopped, dumbstruck, when she saw her; standing in front of one of the shop windows, gazing at a pretty green frock displayed just behind the glass. Her hair was shorter, but it had to be her. It just had to be.

"Mama!" A cry of joy sprang from Fae's lips, erasing all the toil and trauma of the past few days. She broke into a run, then a sprint, throwing herself across the square, her heart racing wildly, her feet slapping on the cobblestones. "Mama, it's you!"

She grabbed Mama's hand, and the woman spun around. A pair of soft brown eyes stared down at her, and they were not Mama's eyes. In fact, she was not Mama at all.

"Are you lost, dear?" the lady asked.

"You're not my mama." Fae backed away, dropping the lady's hand as if it were red hot. "You're not my mama."

She stumbled away, staring around the marketplace in desperation. Where could she be? Then she spotted her, walking across the square, carrying a baby.

"Mama!" she cried again, relieved, and ran toward her. This time the pair of eyes that stared down at her were blue, but they still weren't Mama's.

Fae ran in zigzags across the square from one woman to the

next, crying out in hope, then in desperation, and then in utter panic. Woman after woman spun around to look at her, and woman after woman, was not her mama. It was pitch dark but for the golden puddles of light pooling beneath the street lamps and shopfronts by the time Fae came to a halt in the middle of the square, her heart thundering, tears streaming down her cheeks as she spun slowly and realized Mama was not here.

"No. She *has* to be here. She has to be here somewhere," Fae whispered to herself, wrapping her arms around herself. It was getting colder, and she felt a shudder trace its way down her spine. She closed her eyes, trying her best to remember, to not panic. Mama didn't come to the market every day, did she? She must be at home. Maybe the man was there, and Mama had to spend time with him. Yes, Mama was at home. But where was home?

"Number 57B, Crawley Street," Fae whispered to herself, her words coming out on a little cloud of steam. Mama had made her say it over and over when she was little, memorizing the address so that she would never be lost. But now, the words seemed to leave her more lost than ever, staring around at an unfriendly city.

She began to wonder how big London was as she gazed at the shops lining the square. She remembered the square from when she was little; the sweet shop, the grocer's, the seamstresses', but none of them were here. Instead, there was a butchery and a milliner's and a hatmaker's.

"This isn't our square," Fae murmured, horror dawning in her heart. How many squares were there in London? How many streets? How many houses?

Fae didn't know. All she did know was that there was just one Mama, and she had to find her. She spotted a street sign on the corner of the square and walked up to it, frowning at the letters, trying her best to remember Ollie's gentle voice guiding her through all of the sounds.

"L... Lynn... Lynnwood," she muttered. "Lynnwood Avenue." It didn't sound familiar. She started down the street and saw another sign on the next corner. Not knowing any other way, she wrapped her arms around herself and began to walk toward it, trying not to wonder how many street signs there were in London. And how many of them said Crawley Street.

༺❀༻

Ollie's new brown shoes clipped and clopped most satisfyingly on the frozen earth. His Grandpa had made them for him for Christmas; they were only two days old, and they were the most magnificent things that he'd ever seen. Well, almost the most magnificent. The three books that he cradled in his arms – one from his mother, one from his aunt, and one from his grandmother – were pretty special, too. He couldn't wait to read them, but most of all, he couldn't wait to show them to Fae.

He was giggling in delighted exhilaration as he reached the

hedge and climbed into his hiding spot, which was smoothed down and hollowed out from years of use. Hunkering down on his new shoes, he peered into the branches of the oak tree, wondering if Fae was outside already. But the branches were empty. That was a little strange – it was dusk already; normally, she'd be waiting for him by now. But he wasn't worried. He settled in and, unable to resist the wonderful paper smell of his new books, cracked open the first one and began to read.

He read a page and then looked out at the tree again, but it was still empty. Trying to dispel a flutter of worry, he read another page. Then another. And another. Ollie had finished an entire chapter and it was getting almost too dark to see the words when he finally crawled out of his hiding spot and went up to the tree, walking around it and peering up into the branches from all angles. Where was she?

Worry clawed at his guts now. He looked up at the big house and saw that there was not a single light burning – not a candle, nothing. A cold shiver ran down his spine. Where were her grandparents? Why were they sitting in that dark house? He took a step nearer. The last light of Boxing Day was just enough to sketch out the shrouded-looking silhouette of her grandfather sitting in the armchair in the upper bedroom; they'd often spied on him there from the branches of the tree. Why hadn't he lit a candle?

Ollie ventured a few steps nearer to the house. He was a little frightened of Fae's grandparents, and he knew that their friendship was supposed to be a secret, but he couldn't shake the feeling that something was terribly wrong. Had he made a mistake by not going to see her on Christmas Eve or Christmas Day? It had been too hard to sneak away while his family was so busy with the festivities. He hadn't wanted to get her in trouble.

He didn't want to get her in trouble now, either, but he had to do something. Taking a tentative step closer, he hissed, "Pssst! Fae! Where are you?"

There was no reply. Ollie raised his voice slightly, trying not to sound suspicious. "I lost my ball in your garden!" he shouted. "Will you come and help me look for it?"

Nothing. Nothing even stirred inside the house.

Ollie was scared now. "Fae!" he shouted, loudly.

But the only reply was his own voice bouncing off the lonely eaves in the house and the tall branches of the tree, and it spooked him. Backing away, he stared up at the dark house, and an intense fear crept across the ground toward him like a growing shadow. He didn't know if he should go inside and look for Fae, or call for help, or not do anything at all. All he knew was that he was scared, so he ran.

***

"Excuse me, sir." Fae's voice sounded weak and wrung-out even to her. "Sir?"

The greengrocer who was busy packing his wares into his shop turned around. When he saw her, she saw the same expression that every person she'd asked had given her: disgust. He took a step back, as if worried she might try to grab at his coat with her dirty hands.

"What do you want?" he demanded bluntly.

"Sir, I just want to know if you know Betty Carter," said Fae.

"Never heard of her."

"And do you know where Crawley Street is? Sir? Please, sir!"

But the greengrocer was already walking into his shop, slamming the door behind him. Fae bit her lip, trying to hold back the tide of tears that threatened to overwhelm her. She turned away, spotting the only other person on the street, an old lady who was wobbling down the pavement, dressed in rags. "Ma'am!" Fae ran toward her. "Ma'am, do you know Betty Carter?"

The old lady turned to look at her, and her eyes were just two glowing yellow orbs in her face, devoid of personality or expression. They struck terror like a cold knife into Fae's guts. She backed away, but the old lady came closer, holding out a claw-like hand, and Fae's courage failed her. She turned tail and ran as hard as she could.

She fled from lamplight to lamplight, but she couldn't escape the creeping cold, or the hunger that had started to gnaw a

THE INVISIBLE DAUGHTER

hole in her being. It seemed like an awfully long time since that carrot.

The smell of food wafted through the air toward her. She sucked in the scent as if it could somehow feed her. It seemed to be coming from a shop a little way up the street; there was light inside, and she could hear music, and she could hear voices. They sounded happy.

Desperate, Fae headed toward it.

She was only a few yards from the door when it crashed open. Three young men stumbled out, swaying, hanging on to each other and giggling loosely as they tried to remain upright on the pavement. Fae stopped, staring at them. She wasn't sure what was going on with them, but something about them made a hole open in the pit of her stomach, and it wasn't from hunger.

She was aware of the moment they spotted her. One of them gave a loud laugh that seemed to be part burp in there somewhere. The strange smell rolling off them was fruity and unpleasant, and it worried her.

"Look at th-that," the young man slurred, grabbing at his companion and pointing somewhere to the left of Fae.

Fae didn't want to hear what was going to happen to next. Listening to her instincts, she turned and ran again, and she could hear shouts behind her as they gave chase. Her fear of the dark gave way to her desperation to hide. She plunged down another alleyway and bolted, leaving their strange, stumbling voices far behind.

The cold was not as easy to get rid of, though. She wrapped her arms around herself, picking her way in the dark through the rubbish she couldn't see. Things scuttled and rattled in the shadows, broken glass clinking under her feet. She had to find somewhere warm. Or just keep wandering, forever, in the night. There was no tinker to save her this time.

It felt like the alley had gone on forever when she finally saw the light. She paused, squinting. In the flickering glow, she could see the alley had opened up onto what looked like some disused old yard, but she was more interested in the source of the light. It looked like a fire, and Fae could feel its warmth calling her.

She slunk closer. A few figures were huddled around the light, and she was struck by how small they were. Clinging to the shadows around the edge of the yard, Fae crept nearer until she could hear them talking.

"Joey, Harry, you're going to head over to that posh marketplace where all those pretty ladies like to stare at dresses and leave their purses unattended." The speaker was one of the taller figures who was sitting around the fire. As Fae slipped around the edge of the yard, she could see it was a girl several years older than she was, somewhere in her teens. She had a torrent of thick, dark hair, and an accent that sounded exotic.

"Yes, Rosa," said two of the littler figures obediently.

"Good. That's good. And you, Amy, Eliza, you're going to go to the factories and see if you can drum up any work for us, all right? Just not as match girls. We won't work in those awful places." The older girl sighed.

Fae was close enough now to see the shadows dancing over her face, and how deeply black her eyes were. She looked down at two small children – almost tots – who clung to each other, sharing a blanket at the edge of the fire as they stared up at the older girl in terror.

"And you two, Peggy, Lucas, just try not to get lost or killed. You're going to hide here and behave yourselves and wait for us all to come back."

Fae didn't want to be seen. All she wanted was to feel a little warmth from the fire. She lowered herself into the shadow of a broken box a little way behind the bigger girl, not wanting to be in the firing line of her sharp eyes. She settled down, leaning against the box. Some of the children grouped around the fire were nibbling on bread or using it to scrape out old tins; Fae assumed there had been soup in them. Her stomach growled. She longed for her grandmother's thick pea soup...

"It's going to be a cold night," the older girl was saying. "We'll need to try and scrounge some extra blankets tomorrow. That will be my job. I'm going over to the shipyards – I'll be able to steal something from one of the merchant ships, either blankets or something to sell so that we can get them." Fae saw the girl's hand move to her side. "All that's assuming that our little intruder isn't going to cut our throats as we sleep."

Before Fae could move, metal flashed in the firelight, and the older girl moved like a flashing shadow. In the space of a half breath, the girl was towering over Fae, a knife held above her head, black lightning flashing in her eyes. Fae stumbled back, too frightened to scream; her knees gave way under her and she fell onto her back, staring up at the girl, staring up at the knife.

The moment twanged like a violin string. Then, the girl lowered the knife.

"Why, you're just a little child," she said, surprise and compassion alike creeping into her voice. She tucked the knife into her belt. "I'm impressed. It's not easy to creep up on me."

Fae could barely breathe, let alone speak. The girl crouched down onto her haunches and studied Fae, her eyes calculating now. "Where do you come from, then?"

Fae sat up. "The country," she whispered.

"That's a long way. Don't think I've seen the country since my days in the circus," said the girl. "Are you cold?"

Fae nodded.

"Hungry?"

Fae nodded again.

"You're good at sneaking," said the girl. "We could use someone like you." She held out a hand. "Come on. I'm sure there's some food and fire left for you."

Fae wasn't sure she trusted this exotic-looking girl, but she couldn't deny how wonderful the warmth of the fire was. She reached out and took the girl's hand.

"Thank you," she murmured.

"Manners? That's interesting," said the girl, raising an eyebrow. "Since we're being polite, I'm Rosa."

"Fae Carter."

"Pleased to meet you," said Rosa, with a flamboyant little bow. "Come on. You'll be all right. Don't worry."

But Rosa's words were hard to believe, alone in the city.

Mama had never felt so far away.

CHAPTER 7

"That's all you have to do," Rosa concluded. "For someone who can sneak about like you, it'll be easy as pie."

"Really?" said Fae doubtfully, staring at the crowd of people bustling down the street. They all seemed to be in such a hurry that they barely saw one another, mothers clutching their schoolboys' hands, men walking briskly as they swung their briefcases, a group of young women in a neat little row.

"Absolutely," said Rosa with confidence. "They're all so focused on getting to work on time, they won't even notice you. Look." She touched Fae's arm and pointed to a young gentleman hurrying along the street toward them. He was reading a newspaper as he walked, his umbrella swinging on the crook of his arm. "See the bulge in his pocket? That's a pocket-watch. He's a perfect target."

"I'd rather hide here," said Fae nervously, shrinking a little deeper into their nook between two buildings.

"Come on, Fae," said Rosa. "You've got to contribute somehow if you want to stay with us." She shrugged. "I'm sorry, but I already have Peggy and Lucas who are too young to work, and it's a tight stretch to feed all those hungry mouths. It's snatch that watch, or find some other way to survive."

Fae swallowed hard. She'd been wedged between the sleeping bodies of two of Rosa's other friends all night, and it had still been so cold she barely slept. She knew she wouldn't last more than a day or two on these streets alone.

"All right," she said.

"That's the spirit." Rosa patted the top of Fae's head. "Off you go."

Holding her breath, Fae slipped out into the crowd, staying with the shadows, moving as quietly as she could. She was so used to hiding, to silence. She knew how to remain unnoticed, just as it was easy at the market yesterday morning to move stealthily through the crush of bodies. In a minute, she was half a step behind the young man. He was still so engrossed in his newspaper that he didn't even look up as Fae's hand slipped into his coat pocket and she found a smooth, hard disc inside. She fished it out, and her heart hammered for a terrible instant as the frown deepened on the young man's face. But he just seemed to be even more interested in his paper. He lifted it a few inches closer to his nose, and Fae melted into the crowd, making her way back to the hiding place with Rosa.

"I got it," she panted, holding out the watch to Rosa. It gleamed silver in her palm.

"You little beauty." Rosa swiped the watch out of Fae's hand, and it disappeared somewhere onto her person. "I told you you'd be good at this." She grinned, slapping Fae on the back. "You're a right useful little pickpocket already. We're going to eat well for a few nights now."

Fae looked back into the street. The young man, still reading his paper, slipped one hand into his pocket. He stopped, lowering his paper, and started patting himself down, looking for his watch.

"Oh, he misses it," she said, unhappily.

"That means it's time to get out of here," said Rosa. She grabbed Fae's arm. "Come on! Let's go and sell this to my favorite fence so we can get us some food before we go back to the warehouse."

Fae gave the young man a last, lingering glance as he spun around and began to look up and down the pavement in case he'd dropped his watch. She felt so terrible, yet she knew if she refused to do this again, Rosa would throw her out – and she couldn't think of another way to get food and shelter.

Her heart in her shoes, Fae turned to follow Rosa down the

alley. *Someday I'll make this right,* she promised the young man in her thoughts. *I'll find my mama and I'll pay it all back – someday.*

IT HAD BEEN TOO LONG SINCE FAE HAD GONE. OLLIE STOOD in front of the back door of the house, staring up at it in the misty morning light. The fog that still lay thick across the common seemed to have the landscape in a cold and breathless grip; even the old oak tree was just a haunting shadow in the mist behind him. Even so, Fae should have been outside by now. She never failed to come outside, even if it was raining, just to say hello.

It had been days now since Ollie had last seen her. He closed his eyes, imagining her shining eyes, her rippling laughter. Determination took hold of his heart. He would do anything to make sure she was safe – even go into this great, spooky house with the motionless silhouette of Fae's grandfather still waiting, eerily still, in that high window.

"What if they've done something to her?" he murmured to himself. "I have to find her."

He reached for the doorknob and turned it slowly. When the hinges let out a drawn-out squeal, like some forlorn creature in pain, he jumped back. But the door continued to swing open, revealing a perfectly ordinary kitchen. The cupboard door was open, and so was the bread bin, showing nothing but cobwebs inside; but there was a great bowl of cream on the kitchen table, a few brown paper bags, a wilted cabbage. Ollie ventured inside, his heart in his mouth.

The door to the dining room was open, and Ollie stepped inside, looking around. Everything seemed so undisturbed.

"Fae?" he called out softly.

The word seemed deafening in the deathly stillness; it didn't echo, but Ollie felt the silence in his bones. He swallowed hard. Maybe he should turn back. But maybe Fae was in trouble up there, and he'd promised to be her friend always – even if that meant doing something that scared him.

"Fae?" he called out again, walking toward the staircase at the end of the room. When he began to climb, a board squealed beneath his foot, the sound reverberating through the house. Ollie swallowed.

"Mr. Carter?" he called out. "It's me, Ollie Briggs. I – I just saw that your lights weren't burning." He took another step, chiding himself a little for being so fearful. How frightening could two old people be? "Hello?" he called, reaching the landing. There was only one door slightly ajar on the corridor, so he headed toward it.

"Anyone?" he asked, pushing the door wider.

There was no one in the room. At least, no one Ollie could see. Still, every hair on his body stood suddenly bolt upright. There was a horrible stench in the air. He felt his mouth drying as he stared into the room. There was a double bed there, and an armchair, and there was *something* in each of them. Two figures. And they were both covered with clean white sheets. Curiosity and horror clashed in his brain, and curiosity won. He stepped forward, grabbed the corner of the sheet on the bed with his fingertips, and gave it a quick tug. It fell back and revealed the face of old Mrs. Carter – or what used to be old Mrs. Carter. The skin was blue-gray now, the mouth wide open, and the eyes. They were glazed. Misty. Expressionless.

Dead.

Ollie let out a scream of panic that he hadn't known was in him. He bolted, his feet loud now in the empty house, almost falling down the stairs, crashing back out of the back door and fleeing across the backyard as fast as his legs could carry him. He could feel Mrs. Carter's ghost chasing him all the way down the lane, howling around him in the mist, the fog clinging to his clothes and hands like some deathly specter hot on his heels.

"HELP!" Ollie shrieked, spurred on to greater speed still. He reached the end of the lane, turned hard left onto a sheep path, slipped, fell, righted himself and was running almost before he hit the ground. "MAMA! PAPA! Help me! HELP!"

Blessedly, at last, the familiar shape of the farmhouse where he lived appeared from the mist. Dogs and chickens scattered as Ollie sprinted across the farmyard and crashed through the front door.

"MAMA!" he screamed as loudly as he could.

"Ollie!" Mama dashed out of the kitchen. There was flour on her hands, and her face was almost the same shade of white. She grabbed Ollie's arms. "What is it, darling? Where are you hurt? What's the matter?"

"The Carters," Ollie gasped out, wheezing and shaking with fear. "The Carters. The Carters."

"The Carters?" Mama clutched him. "What about them?"

Ollie's shaking legs gave way under him. He collapsed to the floor, still trembling, and Mama knelt in front of him. Her eyes were searching, frightened. "Ollie, talk to me."

"Fae," Ollie panted. "Her grandparents." His lungs were burning with fear and running. "They're still in there."

"Who is? In where?" asked Mama. "You're as white as a sheet, child. Tell me what's going on."

The front door opened again, and Ollie looked up. Papa's reassuring shape stood in the doorway, tall and strong, vibrant and real. He felt his heart slowing down.

"What is it?" Papa crossed the distance between them in what seemed to be a single long bound. "What's the matter?"

"I don't know," said Mama, laying a hand on Ollie's cheek.

"He just came in here like this, screaming at the top of his lungs."

"Now then, my boy." Papa knelt in front of him, his eyes twinkling kindly. "What's the matter? What's happened?"

Ollie took a deep breath, trying to steady himself. "It's Mr. and Mrs. Carter," he said. "My friend Fae lives there." He knew he was supposed to keep her a secret, but he also knew that someone had to help her. "She's gone. I couldn't find her, so I went into the house, and I found them." He felt another shudder trace its cold fingers down his spine. "They're both dead, Papa. Mr. and Mrs. Carter are both lying dead there."

Mama and Papa exchanged a shocked glance. "Mrs. Willows did tell me that Mrs. Carter fainted at the market a few days ago, James," said Mama.

"I'll go." Papa straightened up. He laid a warm hand on the top of Ollie's head. "I think he needs a little cocoa, don't you?"

Ollie didn't want cocoa. He wanted Fae. Mama sat him down in front of the hearth, swaddled him in blankets, and gave him a hot cup of cocoa so sweet he could smell the sugar as he clutched the mug in both hands. But he didn't take a single sip. Instead, staring into the crackling flames of the hearth, he prayed with all his heart that Fae would be safe.

It seemed to be a long time later when Papa came in again.

Mama, who had been sitting in an armchair behind Ollie with some darning, looked up.

"James?" she said.

"It's true," said Papa, taking off his hat and shaking the snow off. "The undertaker is there now. They're both gone."

"And Fae?" asked Ollie. "Papa, did you find Fae?"

Papa frowned. "Who's Fae?"

"Their granddaughter, Papa. She's only ten. She's my friend," said Ollie. "She's supposed to be a secret, but I don't know where she is now. I don't know what's happened to her."

"Ollie, darling," said Mama softly, laying a hand on his shoulder. "Mr. and Mrs. Carter didn't have a granddaughter. Their only child, Betty, died a few years ago."

"That's not true, Mama," Ollie insisted. "Betty is Fae's mama. She lives in the city, and she sent Fae to live with Mr. and Mrs. Carter more than four years ago."

"I know this is a terrible shock, darling." Mama kissed his forehead.

"We have to find her, Mama," Ollie pleaded. "We've got to find Fae."

"Shhh now. It's just the shock, my dear," said Mama. "You'll feel better in the morning."

Ollie knew it was useless to argue. Mama and Papa thought

Fae was imaginary, but Ollie knew she was real. He stared into the flames, his heart aching, sure of one thing: no matter who believed him, he was going to find Fae.

No matter what.

※

AMY AND ELIZA HAD FOUND AN ABANDONED WAREHOUSE when they'd been looking for work in the factory district earlier that day. Rosa had immediately deemed it the perfect place to stay, and now Fae was lying on its cold floor, staring up at the high roof. There was a shingle missing right near the top, and she could see the stars through that – or at least, some of the stars. They seemed grubby and faded in comparison with the dazzling constellations she used to see through the window of her tiny room back in the country.

It felt so far away now. Fae pulled the thin blanket Rosa had given her a little closer around her shoulders, shifting slightly between the slumbering bodies of the two smallest children – Peggy and Lucas. Their presence was comforting, yet somehow, with everyone so soundly asleep, Fae felt intensely lonely.

She wondered if heaven was somewhere beyond those stars and if Grandma and Grandpa were living there now. Mama always said that good people went to heaven if they believed in God. Fae wasn't sure that Grandma had been such a good person, but she hoped that she'd gotten to go to heaven, because Grandpa had loved her so much. Of course, he would have gone to heaven, but he would hate it there if Grandma couldn't come, too.

Maybe Mama was in heaven, too. Maybe Rosa had been right. As they'd walked toward the warehouse, carrying their scant belongings, Fae had asked her if she knew where Crawley Street was.

"Crawley?" Rosa had shaken her head. "Not sure, but it sounds rather posh. It won't be down here in this part of town. Why?"

"My mama lives there," said Fae.

"I thought you came from the country."

"I did. I lived there with my grandparents, but they died, so I came here looking for Mama."

Kindness crept into Rosa's sharp eyes. Her voice was gentle. "When last did you see your mama, Fae? And where's your papa?"

"I don't have a papa," said Fae. "It's always just been me and Mama. She sent me to live with my grandparents four years ago because the man who owns our house didn't like me."

"I see," said Rosa. She spoke carefully, putting a gentle hand on Fae's shoulders. "Fae, let me be honest with you. Your mama has probably forgotten all about you by now." She smiled, a little sadly. "It's best you do the same and forget about her, too. Even if she is still alive, if she never spoke to you for four years, she probably just doesn't want you."

"Doesn't want me?" Fae's heart hurt. The thought had occurred to her many times ever since she'd first been sent to the country, but now it seemed far too real. "Then what will I do?"

"Stay with us." Rosa put her arm around Fae's shoulders. "We'll be your family. Forget about her and live your own life with us."

Fae wasn't sure she wanted to live her own life – or believe Mama had forgotten her. She was only ten years old, after all. She stared at the stars, remembering how Mama's eyes could be just as bright on the rare occasions when she smiled. She'd smiled at Fae so often. Maybe she did still love her even though there was something so wrong with her. Either way, Fae couldn't bear not knowing. She would keep searching for Mama until she knew for sure.

She wished Ollie was with her to help her. Closing her eyes, she imagined what he would do if he were here. He'd pull her to her feet and tell her they'd find her mama no matter what. He always said that kind of thing.

"Fae?"

Fae opened her eyes. Peggy was sitting up beside her, two trails of tears running down her cheeks.

"What's the matter, Peggy?" asked Fae, her heart going out to the little girl.

"I'm so scared. May I lie with you?"

Fae was scared too. She opened her arms, and Peggy silently crept into them, pillowing her tiny head on Fae's shoulder.

"Can I come too?" On the other side of Fae, Lucas, Peggy's younger brother, was sitting up. His hair was tousled with sleep, but his eyes were wide and fearful.

"Of course, you can," said Fae.

Lucas crept closer and clambered over his sister, wedging himself between Peggy and Fae. Fae wrapped her arms around the two soft little bodies, cuddling them close to her heart. She closed her eyes and leaned her head on top of theirs, listening as their breathing grew slow and deep. She hadn't realized how much she had missed Edith. For the first time since she'd said goodbye to her baby sister, Fae felt the stirring of a kind of kinship in her heart.

Maybe Rosa was right. Maybe she'd have to find her family right here, right now. But until she knew for sure, Fae promised herself, she wouldn't rest until she'd found her Mama – and her real baby sister.

CHAPTER 8

Two Years Later

"Come on, Peggy!" Fae laughed as she struggled with the wriggling little girl, trying to stuff an errant arm into the sleeve of her ragged little dress. "Hold still!"

"I'm too excited, Fae," laughed Peggy. She peered up at Fae with one brilliantly blue eye, the other obscured by the neck of the dress, which was only halfway pulled over her head.

Fae smiled. "Why?"

"Because today I'm going to sing my new song for the crowd for the first time," said Peggy. "Then you and Rosa are going to get lots of money, and Rosa said if it was good, she would buy me a sticky bun just for me."

"Sticky buns are wonderful," said Fae, "but you're not going to get one if you don't sing your song, and you can't sing your song only half-dressed, you silly."

Despite the fit of giggles that Peggy immediately dissolved into, Fae succeeded in getting her into her dress. It was faded now, but its color still brought out the blue of Peggy's eyes. Fae smiled, smoothing the dress down, and touched the little girl's plump cheek.

"There," she said. "Look how lovely you are."

"Thank you, Fae." Peggy gave a happy little twirl. "I'm so glad you came," she added, more quietly. "I like it lots better when you're here."

"I'm glad I came, too," said Fae. She straightened up and took Peggy's hand. "Come on – let's get going. Where's Lucas?"

"He's over here," came a slightly irritated voice from the other end of the warehouse. It was punctuated by a stream of delighted giggles, and Fae looked up to see Rosa walking across the warehouse toward them. Her face and voice were frowning, but her eyes shone with laughter, and she held Lucas like a sack of flour over her shoulder. He screamed and kicked his legs in the air.

"This little rascal thought he could climb to the top of that heap of rubbish," said Rosa, jerking her head toward a heap of broken old pallets and bits of machinery, relics from when this abandoned warehouse still held something of more value than a bunch of street urchins forgotten by society.

"Lucas!" Fae scolded as Rosa plopped the little boy onto the floor. "How many times have I told you not to go trying to climb up that heap? You'll hurt yourself!"

Lucas stared up at Fae with angelic brown eyes. His tousled black hair flopped half over his eyes, which only heightened the effect.

"Sorry, Fae," he said.

Fae knew he wasn't. "Oh, Lucas," she said. "Don't you think there's enough adventure in our lives without adding to it by this kind of thing, too?"

"I dunno," said Lucas.

"Sometimes he sounds like a four-year-old idiot," said Rosa, though not unkindly. "Now come along. We need to catch the breakfast crowd at the marketplace if you want that sticky bun of yours, Peggy."

Fae took Peggy's and Lucas' hands and held them firmly as she followed Rosa out of the warehouse and up the street. Factory workers blundered past them, glassy-eyed, seeming not to notice them, although a few of the young men did pause to let their eyes wander up and down Rosa's lanky figure, dwelling on the black hair that streamed free in the breeze.

Rosa didn't seem to notice them, even though Fae thought

she herself would be terrified if someone looked at her in that way. She simply led Fae and the smaller children out of the factory district and into the more affluent streets where the marketplace was located. They paused behind a cart piled high with merchandise so Fae could smooth down Peggy's hair and tie a ribbon in the end of each pigtail.

"Now, remember your words nicely, and don't forget to look all the women in the eye sometimes," Rosa coached her. "We'll be going after their necklaces, so it's important that they keep watching you all the time."

"Can I do a handstand, Rosa?" asked Lucas.

"That's not part of your dance," said Rosa.

"I know, but I like doing handstands."

"Maybe next time, all right?" Rosa smiled. "Are you ready?"

"Yes!" Peggy skipped in place, clapping her little hands together.

For a moment, Fae thought of how strange and how awful it was that seven-year-old Peggy would be so excited about what they were about to do. A crushing awareness of how she'd been surviving for the past two years descended upon her. They'd been stealing – she and Rosa and all of the other older children in the group – and these two innocent little children had been helping them to do just that. They knew it, but did they realize what it was that they were doing? Did they know it was wrong?

What would Grandma have said?

And what would Mama say once Fae finally found her? Fae felt her palms begin to sweat. Would Mama throw her away again because she was a thief?

"Fae? Hello?" Rosa waved a hand in front of Fae's eyes.

"Sorry," said Fae, dragging her thoughts away from that dark place. "What?"

"I asked if you're ready."

Fae shook herself, looking down at Peggy and Lucas. Right or wrong, they had to eat, and she couldn't find another way of doing that without stealing. The workhouse was an intolerable thought. "Yes, I'm ready."

"Good." Rosa gave Peggy a little push toward the crowd. "Off you go, then."

Peggy extended a hand to Lucas, who took it. Together, closely watched by Fae and Rosa, they walked across to the street corner they'd scouted out the day before. Peggy took her place a couple of steps behind Lucas, whose little face was furrowed with concentration as he tried to remember his dance.

Fae saw Peggy's shoulders lift as she took a deep breath and began to sing, carefully enunciating the words.

"Seated one day at the organ, I was weary and ill at ease," she sang, "and my fingers wandered idly over the noisy keys..."

That was Lucas's cue. With the kind of energy only a little boy could muster, he began to dance. His little feet were light on the pavement, his body twisting and bending in time with the song in a way that made it seem as if he was not just a little boy dancing but the melody itself made flesh.

"Thank goodness for that child's rhythm," grunted Rosa. "Come on, Fae. Let's go."

A crowd was beginning to gather to watch the children. Fae saw a faint blush come to Peggy's cheeks, but knew that she liked an audience – the bigger, the better. She swelled her little chest with as deep a breath as she could take and pushed her voice to a higher pitch.

"I know not what I was playing, or what I was dreaming then. But I struck one chord of music like the sound of a great Amen! Like the sound of a great Amen!"

Peggy's voice rang through the crowd, and the lady standing nearest to Fae leaned closer, her eyes wide, hands clasped by her chest as she was engrossed in the sound of the little girl singing. Fae saw her moment. Slipping past, her fingertips just barely touching it, she opened the little clasp of the gold chain that the lady wore around her neck. The chain tumbled flee, brushing the lady's arm, but she was listening too closely to Peggy to notice. Fae scooped it into her pocket and moved deeper into the crowd.

"It flooded the crimson twilight like the close of an angel's psalm, and it lay on my fevered spirit with a touch of infinite calm," sang Peggy.

Among the crush of bodies, Fae spotted Rosa. She was tucking a watch into her pocket, and when their eyes met, she gave a faint nod. They had what they needed – it was time to disappear before Peggy finished her song. As Fae made her way through the crowd toward Rosa, she heard a gasp and a ripple of laughter from the gathered people. Lucas must have done his handstand after all – he was lucky he'd pulled it off.

"I have sought, but I seek it vainly, that one lost chord divine, which came from the soul of the organ and entered into mine," Peggy's voice rose above the sound of the murmuring crowd. Fae stepped to the side to avoid a gentleman who was turning around, and when she looked up again, she realized that she couldn't see Rosa anymore. Puzzled, she stopped, looking around for that black mane among the pale colors of the ladies' dresses. Where could she be?

Peggy's voice was rising, gathering strength as she reached the crescendo of the song. "It may be that death's bright angel will speak that chord again; it may be that only in Heav'n, I shall hear that great – ROSA!"

Peggy's shriek was discordant, a shattering of the magical music of her voice. Fae spun around. Had someone seized her? But Peggy was still on her street corner, her pigtails streaming onto her shoulders, her eyes wide. She was staring, horrified, into the crowd.

"Rosa!" she shrieked again.

"Stop!" Lucas straightened up, balling his tiny hands into fists. "Let her go!"

Fae whipped around. Horror filled her when she spotted Rosa, pinned between two policemen, one of which had his hand over her mouth so she couldn't cry out. She was struggling hard, her slender legs kicking, but she was no match for the two burly men.

"Rosa!" Fae screamed, running toward her.

Rosa's struggles slowed. Her eyes flashed above the rough fingers of the policeman holding her, and Fae saw her bite down. The policeman howled in pain and jerked his hand back. Rosa planted her elbow in his belly and tried to wrench free of the other man, but his grip was iron.

"Let go of her! Let her go! We need her!" Fae yelled.

"No! Fae! Stop!" shouted Rosa.

Her authoritative voice brought Fae skidding to a halt. She watched in horror as the policeman grabbed hold of Rosa's arm again. Rosa kicked him in the knees, still screaming. "Get the children! Get them and get out of here before they grab you!"

Fae took a step back, spotting another policeman across the marketplace. The crowd so recently enraptured by Peggy's singing was watching Rosa's arrest with just as much interest, but this policeman's eyes were resting on Fae. Her gut twisted. She couldn't let anything happen to the little ones.

"Go, Fae!" roared Rosa. "Go and get to somewhere—"

"Shut up, you wench!" snapped the policeman, and his bloodied hand slapped over Rosa's face with ringing force. Fae screamed as Rosa went limp in their arms, and they began to drag her away. She wanted so much to run toward her, to fight to free her.

"Fae!"

The voice behind her was terrified. Fae spun around to see Peggy and Lucas clinging to each other, staring up at the other policeman, who was walking purposefully toward them. She gave one last glance at Rosa's limp form and then ran toward the little ones, her body trembling with fear.

"Come on!" Fae scooped Lucas into her arms and grabbed Peggy's hand. "Let's go!"

"What about Rosa?" begged Lucas, tears streaming down his cheeks.

"She told us to go. We've got to go!" shouted Fae.

Then they were running, Lucas bouncing on Fae's hip, Peggy being half-dragged behind her as she fled as fast as her legs could carry her. Down the long street, out of the posh district, toward the factories. At some point, the pounding feet of their pursuers melted into the distance, but Fae didn't stop running until they had tumbled into their warehouse and collapsed to the floor, panting and gasping.

Fae lay on her back, clutching the two little ones, her heart hammering painfully in her chest. She could hear both Peggy and Lucas sobbing against her.

"What are we going to do, Fae?" Peggy was the first to sit up. She'd lost a ribbon, and her hair stood in all directions, made wild by the running. "What are we going to do without Rosa?"

"I don't know, Peggy." Fae felt tears fill her own eyes and pulled Peggy close to her. "I just don't know."

***

THE CROWN OF THE OLD OAK TREE WAS TOPPED WITH vibrant greenery as it towered over the old house, a timeless study in majesty and splendor. Ollie wondered if it had grown in the two years since he had last tried to climb it. It must have, but he'd been here every day to see it and hadn't noticed. Would he notice now, if he vaulted onto one of those lower branches and started scrambling from bough to bough? Would it be harder to get to the top, or had he grown in proportion to the tree? Would it be higher than the last time he'd been cradled in its canopy? Would he be able to see even further than before?

Would he be able to see all the way to wherever Fae was now?

He sighed, laying a hand on the bark of the tree. He remembered lying here beneath its shady branches so often on a summery afternoon, giggling with Fae, the smell of crushed grass rising up all around him. It had been two years, but he still couldn't believe that she was somehow just gone.

"Ollie! What are you doing?"

Ollie turned. His brother, Otis, was standing at the bottom of the garden and waiting for him. "Papa wants us in the hay field, remember?" Otis shouted. "Hurry up!"

"I know! I know," said Ollie. "I'm coming." He reluctantly lifted his hand off the bark, one finger at a time, and then turned to approach his brother.

Otis's arms were folded. He had the same serious gray eyes as Papa, but they still held something teasing, just like when he and his friends used to pick on Ollie for reading books when he could have been playing at knights. "What were you doing in there, Ollie?" he asked. "Daydreaming about your imaginary girl?"

"Fae wasn't imaginary. She's real. I know she's real," said Ollie.

"Then how come I never saw her?" mocked Otis.

"Because she was a secret, Otis. I don't know why." Ollie sighed. "I should have asked why, but I was just a little child when I first met her. I should have found out more. I should have protected her." He bit his lip. "Then maybe she'd be safe now."

"There was never any little girl living there," said Otis. "Really, Ollie, I know it was frightening to find those two old people dead in that house, but you have to accept that it was all your imagination."

"I know it wasn't," said Ollie insistently. "I knew her for four years. She was my friend." He gritted his teeth. "She *is* my friend, and I'll find her one day."

Otis stopped, facing his brother. He put a hand on Ollie's shoulder, real concern flashing over his face. "You've got to stop this, Ollie. It's been two years. You can't spend the rest of your life longing for someone who never existed – and even if she did, she's long gone. There was no little girl in that house. Just two grumpy old people who weren't nice to anyone, and now that they're gone, it's been a stroke of luck for us because we get to have the farm." He shrugged. "I know it's harsh, but you have to forget her."

Otis turned sharply and headed off toward the hay field. Ollie followed, slowly, feeling as if his heart was almost too heavy to carry. He knew his brother's words were spoken in concern, but they were still daggers through his heart – because he just couldn't give up on Fae. He couldn't let her go.

He would never let her go.

❦

Fae was too afraid to stay in the warehouse. If she

did, she would have to tell all the other children what had happened to Rosa – and they would all know that it had been her fault. She'd lost their leader, their hope, and their protection. Maybe the other children would beat her or throw her into the river. Maybe she deserved it; she had started to think, after two years of being part of the strange little family that Rosa had built, that perhaps whatever was wrong with her had healed or gone away somehow. But now she knew for sure that there was something terrible about her, something that she had to hide. She'd killed her grandparents, she'd gotten Rosa arrested, and she'd even driven Ollie away. Now, there was no one left.

No one except for Peggy and Lucas. And Fae knew she had to get rid of them, too, quickly, before something awful happened to them the way it had to everyone else she'd ever loved.

"You just stay here," she said repeatedly, tucking the two children up in a blanket by the fire. She'd struggled to strike the flint with her trembling hands, but now at least it was warming up the warehouse. She prayed no one would see the smoke and come to find them. "Just stay here for me, all right?"

"Where did they take Rosa?" Peggy asked, tears still running down her cheeks. "When is she coming back?"

"I don't know, Peggy." Fae swallowed hard, knowing Rosa was never coming back. "I don't know."

"Why did they take her?" asked Lucas. "Were we doing something wrong?"

His words wrenched at Fae's heart. "No, darling, no." She bent to kiss his forehead, brushing aside his messy curls. "You did nothing wrong. It's not your fault." *It's mine*, she added silently. "Now you're going to just sit here and wait nicely until the others get back. Amy and Eliza will probably be here soon."

"But where are you going?" asked Peggy.

Fae didn't know. "I... I guess I'll find out," she said.

"And when are *you* coming back?" asked Lucas.

Fae stared down into his pleading eyes. She wanted to tell him not to want her so badly, that there was something wrong with her, that if he stayed near her, something terrible was sure to happen to him. But she couldn't find the words.

"I don't know," she said.

"Fae, you can't go." Peggy's little hand shot out, grabbing the sleeve of Fae's dress. "You can't go, too. Rosa's gone." She swallowed a sob. "We need you."

"No, you don't." Fae snatched back her arm. "You've got the other children. You'll be fine."

"No!" Lucas pushed away the blanket and lunged at Fae, seizing her skirt in both hands. "We need *you* – not Rosa, not the others. We need you, Fae!"

Fae's heart felt like it would explode in her chest with agony. Tears blurred her vision as she grabbed Lucas' fists, but they were gripping her dress so tightly that she knew she wouldn't be able to pry them loose. She opened her mouth, wanting to tell them to stay, that they couldn't follow her. Yet the fear in Lucas' eyes stopped her. She took a deep breath.

"All right," she choked out past the tears filling her throat. "Let's go."

The children didn't ask where they were going. They just clutched Fae's hands and followed her, close as chicks under a hen's wings, out into the street.

She didn't know where she was going. She just took the most unfamiliar routes she could find, terrified of bumping into one of the other children. Peggy and Lucas were completely silent beside her as they wandered on, passing factory after factory. The smells coming from those places were appalling – some were smoky, some rotting, some with the harsh, acrid stench of unknown chemicals. Fae thought of going into one of them and asking for work there, but then she remembered Rosa's stories about the match girls whose faces rotted clean away, and she was too scared to go inside.

Dusk found them in an alleyway, huddled together against the insidious cold that seeped deeper and deeper into their bones. Fae wrapped Peggy and Lucas up in her arms, holding them in her lap, but she could feel their little bodies shaking. They were out of the factory district now, and the street that Fae could see through the opening of the alleyway was alight and bustling; the well-dressed men and women walking by were laughing and joking, jewels glinting on brooches and necklaces and rings. A delicious smell floated tantalizingly toward them from the nearby eating-house, and Fae could hear bursts of laughter emanating from inside.

"Fae, I'm hungry," whispered Lucas, raising his face up to hers. It was smeared with dirt, tears making two clean trails down his cheeks.

"I know." Fae cuddled him closer, her heart thumping with fear. "I know."

"What are we going to do?" asked Peggy. "How are we going to eat?"

"Who's going to take care of us?" asked Lucas.

Fae lowered her head, the weight of their little lives hanging on her shoulders like two giant boulders. They were depending on her, and she didn't know what to do. She felt like a tiny girl watching her grandparents die all over again.

The memory stirred something in her heart. Fae sat up. She wasn't going to let that happen again – not now, and not ever.

"We're going to find a way to survive," she said, surprised by the determination in her own voice. "We're going to be all right."

"But how, Fae?" asked Peggy. "Who will help us?"

Fae closed her eyes, a bittersweet memory filling her mind. Mama. Her soft hands, her warm cooking, her laughter as she played with Edith... Fae hadn't come to London to be part of a group of street children, no matter how happy she had been with Rosa and the others. She'd come here to find her mama. And it was high time she did exactly that.

"My mama will help us," she said, opening her eyes. "I know she will."

"Your mama?" Lucas's eyes widened. "But you've been looking for her for two years. How will you ever find her?"

Fae didn't want to admit to him that she hadn't really been looking for Mama for the past year. She'd felt so safe with Rosa. Now she didn't have a choice anymore. "I don't need to find her. I just need to find her street," said Fae, her voice gathering strength. "Crawley Street. I used to just walk from one street sign to the other, but I know now that London is far too big for that. What I need to do is get a map."

"A map?" Lucas frowned. "Where will you find that?"

Fae stared into the street, hoping for inspiration. Her eyes rested on a young couple who stood arm-in-arm beneath a lamppost. They were dressed simply, and Fae immediately realized they weren't Londoners. When they turned around, the young man was pointing up the street, and she spotted it in the young woman's hands: a map.

"There." Fae pointed. "They must be from out of town. That's how they're finding their way."

"How are we going to get it?" asked Peggy.

"Just be patient." Fae's heart was pounding.

After a few minutes' deliberating, the young couple headed on up the street. As they walked, the young man folded up the map and put it in his back pocket. Fae grinned.

"Stay here," she hissed. Pushing the children off her lap, she scampered out into the street.

Falling into the crowd a few steps behind the couple, Fae felt a pang of remorse as she listened to their conversation. They were happy and excited, she heard as she crept closer and closer to them, always sticking with the shadows. They were on honeymoon from their country estate, and they were so wrapped up in each other, the young woman gazing up at her husband's eyes, her face alight with laughter.

Fae felt a pang of longing, wondering what it would be like to have someone she could stare up to in that way. Ollie's face flitted across her mind. She felt a hitch in her step, the memory so powerful that it made her tremble. But she didn't have time to hesitate. Pulling herself together, she swiped the map out of the young man's pocket; he was so busy gazing into his wife's eyes that he never noticed.

Peggy and Lucas were still waiting in the alleyway, wide-eyed and clinging to each other, when Fae hurried up to them.

"Here," she panted, holding out the map.

"Yes!" Peggy cheered. "Now what do we do?"

Fae sat down, cross-legged, and the children tumbled into her lap as she unfolded the paper. Her heart sank for a moment as she stared at it. There were so many streets, so many names printed in tiny text.

But she couldn't give up now. She didn't have a choice.

"Now we look for Crawley Street," she said, as bravely as she could. "And then we go and find my mama."

CHAPTER 9

Crawley Street had been bigger in Fae's dreams.

She stood on the corner, the map crumpled in her shaking hands, as she stared at the row of houses facing onto the bare, wide street. The sun was warm and kindly on the little green gardens in front of each home, the gardens where Fae had never been allowed to play in case the man saw her if he came for a surprise visit. The gardens were where all those other children had always been playing, where Fae had longed to go. Once, the square of green grass outside of Fae and Mama's home had seemed like the biggest thing in the whole world. But now each garden seemed puny, hardly big enough to hold one-half of a game of tag with Ollie under the branches of the great oak tree.

She knew it was the right street not only because of the name on the sign above her head but because she recognized the colors of the houses; a brick one on the very end, then one painted all in green – a chipped and faded green now, six years later – and then the gray one where she had lived with Mama and Edith. It had seemed so large, so grand back then. It had been Fae's world. But now she could see that it was just a small townhouse with four windows in the front: one for the dining room and one for the kitchen on the ground floor, and just above them, one for Fae's room and one for Mama's. It looked so little.

But it also looked like home.

"Fae? Fae!" Lucas tugged at her hand.

She blinked, looking down at him. "Sorry, Lucas. What did you say?"

"Are we here?" Lucas' expression was eager, his eyes wide. "Is this the right street?"

"Is this your home?" asked Peggy.

Fae swallowed. "Yes," she said softly. She pointed at the gray house with its lavender-painted door and window-frames. "That's my home."

"Is that where your mama lives?" asked Lucas.

"Yes, Mama and my little sister, Edith."

"A little sister!" Peggy's eyes widened. "How old is she, Fae? Will she play with me?"

Fae swallowed, realizing how many years it had been since she last saw Mama. "She's six," she told Peggy. "She'd love to play with you."

"Oh, it's going to be so wonderful!" cried Peggy. "I've never lived in a house before."

"It's going to be so nice in your mama's house," said Lucas.

"It's not Mama's house." Fae paused. Suddenly, she wondered if this was going to be as easy as she'd thought. What would the man say?

"Whose house is it, then?" asked Peggy.

"It's... a man's," said Fae, not knowing what to say. Who was that man to Mama, anyway? He wasn't her husband. He wasn't Fae's papa. But who was he? Why did they stay there with him? Questions Fae had never thought about before began to descend on her, threatening to crush her, loud and heavy and completely unanswerable.

"Let's go," said Lucas, tugging at Fae's hand. "Let's go and see your mama."

"What does she look like?" asked Peggy. "Is she kind? Is she beautiful?"

Fae struggled to get her thoughts back under control. She'd found Crawley Street. Everything was going to be fine.

"She's very kind," she told Peggy. "And she's lovely. She has warm, blue eyes and dark brown hair, and she loves to wear pink, and..."

"Like that lady?" asked Lucas, pointing.

Fae looked up, and there she was. *Mama.* Walking down the street, her hair bobbing on her shoulders, a few streaks of gray in it that weren't there before; but her eyes were the same, and the way she walked was the same, and her smile was the same as she gazed down at the little girl who was holding her hand. The girl was about the same age as Peggy, and she had Mama's blue eyes. Her blonde hair was tied up in two little pigtails with ribbons in them, and she skipped along beside Mama, giggling.

"Edith," Fae whispered and gasped.

"What?" asked Peggy.

"That's Edith," she said. "That's my sister. That's my baby sister." She pulled her hands away from Peggy and Lucas. "That's my mama. That's my mama! Mama! *Mama!*"

Fae's arms and legs seemed half paralyzed with fear for a moment as Mama looked up and her eyes found Fae. Then they suddenly came back to life, and Fae was running, shouting Mama's name, her arms held out, feeling so electrified with joy and excitement that she felt almost disconnected from her body. She could almost see herself running toward Mama, hear herself screaming out. She saw Mama look up.

And she saw her expression change from surprise to something that Fae hadn't been expecting.

It wasn't joy. It was abject terror.

The look of fear in Mama's eyes was strong enough that Fae skidded to a halt, half a step from her. With a shock, Fae realized that she was looking her mother in the eye, instead of looking up at her.

There was a moment of complete silence. Edith was hiding behind Mama, and her gentle whimper of fear was the only sound for a few breathless seconds.

Then Mama's lips parted. She seemed to squeeze the word out from empty lungs.

"Fae?" she whispered.

"Yes, Mama. It's me. It's me, Fae. Your daughter," Fae gasped. Hot tears were coursing down her cheeks. "I've missed you so much. I've been looking for you for so long."

"It's really you." Mama reached up as if to touch Fae's face, then hesitated, drawing her hand back. Her face was ashen. "I thought I'd seen a ghost."

"I'm not a ghost, Mama." Fae grabbed Mama's hand. "It's me. I'm real. I came here to find you." Her voice cracked. "I came looking for you."

"But why?" asked Mama. "I sent you to stay with your grandparents. You would have been safe here. Why did you come back to this place?"

Fae paused, suddenly realizing that she had to tell Mama something terrible. "Mama..." She swallowed. "Grandma and Grandpa are dead."

Mama's eyes widened, instantly filling with tears. "How?" she asked, with simple horror.

Fae backed away, more tears running down her cheeks. How could she tell her mama the truth? How could she tell Mama that she'd killed her own grandparents?

"Th-they got sick," she stammered out. "Mama, I'm so sorry. I tried to save them. I tried to tell them. But they g-g-got sick, and they died, and I should have done something, but I didn't know..."

"Shhh." Mama took an instinctive step forward, reaching out. Her hand grasped Fae's shoulder, and suddenly Fae felt anchored in her storm. She stopped, her breaths slowing.

"I didn't know, Fae," said Mama. "Nobody told me."

"I came here to find you," Fae said again. "I didn't know where else to go."

"Fae?" whispered Peggy's voice behind Fae.

Fae turned. Peggy and Lucas were standing right behind her, clutching each other. "Hush, Peggy," she said.

It was too late. Fae turned back to Mama, and the expression in her eyes had changed. There was a hardness in it now.

"Who are they?" Mama demanded.

"I found them on the street, Mama. We lived together for two years. They're only little. They need me," said Fae.

"Two *years?*" Mama paused. "You've been in London for two years? How did you survive?"

Fae didn't know what to say. "We... we did what we had to," she whispered, tears filling her eyes again.

"Oh, Fae." Mama's eyes filled with pain. "I didn't mean for this to happen." She shook her head.

"Please, Mama." Fae reached for her mother's hand again, grasping it. "Please. Let us come and stay with you."

Mama yanked her hand back as if she'd been burned. "*Us?*" she cried. "These two, as well?"

"Please, Mama." Panic rose in Fae's chest. "Please, we don't have anywhere else to go. We don't have any food. We don't have anywhere to stay. We don't have any friends anymore. We need you, Mama. Please!" Fae's voice was rasping with fear. "Please, Mama, we need you."

"No. Absolutely not," said Mama, backing away. Edith clung to her skirts. "Don't you remember how angry Geoffrey was, Fae?"

"Geoffrey?" Fae was utterly confused.

"Edith's father," said Mama. "Don't you remember how he wanted to hurt you? To hurt Edith?" She put a protective hand on Edith's shoulder. "I won't allow it. It'll only cause trouble, Fae. You know that. *You know that.*"

"But Mama, what am I going to do?" Fae cried. "Oh, please, Mama, you can't leave us here on the street." She felt her knees buckling with the force of her dismay and sank down onto the street, blind with weeping. "Mama, please, please. Don't do this."

In the pause, all that Fae heard was her own quiet sobbing. Peggy and Lucas were behind her, silent and appalled.

"Oh, Fae." Mama knelt down in front of her, and her soft hands pulled Fae's hands away from her face. She wiped the tears from Fae's cheeks, and Fae saw that her expression was utterly broken. "I never meant for this to happen. I thought you would be safe with them." She hung her head, and her shoulders slumped as she appeared to reach a decision. "Very well. You can come home with me. But only you," she added, her tone harsh. "Not the others. Geoffrey will never allow it."

"Mama..." Fae began.

"Do you want them to be thrown into the workhouse, Fae?" Mama's words were as harsh as a slap. "Because if Geoffrey finds them, that is exactly what will happen."

Fae looked back at the two little ones, her heart breaking. She knew she couldn't let that happen to them.

"No," she whispered.

"Then you'll find somewhere to leave them now and come back to the house within the hour," said Mama sharply. She rose to her feet, pulling Fae up beside her. "Only you, Fae, do you understand? Not these two. There's no way you can do that."

Fae gave them one more look, seeing the tears in their eyes. She knew she didn't have a choice, but when she said, "Yes, Mama," it still felt like betrayal.

***

THE ALLEYWAY A SMALL DISTANCE DOWN THE STREET WAS at least a little cleaner than those Fae had grown used to back in the factory district. She opened the cloth bag that contained everything they owned and pulled out a threadbare blanket, spreading it on the ground behind a bunch of broken old barrels. Her tears dripped onto the blanket as she smoothed it down.

"Here." She gasped, her sentences broken up by sobs. "Just sit here. Just stay here and you'll be safe."

"No," screamed Lucas, grabbing Fae's arm. "No, Fae, don't go! Don't leave us!"

"Oh, Lucas, I have to." Fae pried him loose. "I don't have a choice."

"But what will we do?" sobbed Peggy. "How are we going to live?"

"I'll come here every single day," said Fae. "I'll bring you food and everything you need every day. You won't be alone, Peggy."

This seemed to calm the children a little. They huddled down onto the blanket, still clinging to one another as Fae bundled them up in it. She was trying her best to hold back her tears, but they were still threatening just behind her eyelashes.

"It's not forever," she whispered, tucking the blanket tightly around Lucas' shoulders. "I just have to get myself into Geoffrey's good graces, then I'll be able to come back for you and bring you home."

"Do you really think you'll be able to take us home, Fae?" whispered Lucas.

"Yes, I do," said Fae. Doubt fluttered in her heart, but she crushed it ruthlessly. If she didn't believe this, she would never be able to leave the children here. "I just have to show Geoffrey how good and quiet and useful I am, that's all. Then I'm going to bring you into the nice, warm house with plenty of food to eat and a nice fire in the hearth every single night. Mama will come to love you, I know she will, and you'll get to play with Edith, and maybe I'll even teach you your letters."

"That sounds nice," said Peggy, sniffing.

"It is nice. It's going to be lovely." Fae knelt down and planted a kiss on each of the two cold little foreheads.

"Please don't leave us here alone tonight," Lucas whimpered. His eyes were limpid with fear. "We need you, Fae. You can't leave us here."

"I have to, Lucas," said Fae. "This is the only way I can take care of you." She swallowed hard at the lump in her throat. "I'm doing the best I can."

Peggy laid her tiny, chubby hand against Fae's cheek. Her sweet eyes were filled with concern. "Don't cry, Fae," she said. "Please don't cry."

It was very hard not to cry as Fae straightened up and gave the children the last remaining scraps of the food they'd managed to pilfer over the past few days on the street. She watched them tear hungrily at the stale bread and hard cheese, praying she was doing the right thing for them. She couldn't bear to think she was hurting them somehow.

"You stay right here now, all right?" she told them. "I'll be back in the morning."

"Promise?" whispered Lucas.

Fae nodded firmly. "I promise."

Walking away from the alleyway was one of the hardest things Fae had ever done. It was less than a block to the house where Mama lived – her home now, Fae supposed – and yet it seemed just as long as that cold, cold walk on Boxing Day two years ago in the country. She thought of Ollie, and her heart longed for him. She wished she could tell him everything. She wished she had never walked away from him, that he'd come out to her as she waited for him in the tree. Everything would have been better if only Ollie had been there.

But Ollie wasn't here. Just Fae, and the distant sounds of the two children sobbing all alone. She squared her shoulders, forcing herself to take every step until she reached the threshold of Mama's house.

"Mama?" Fae whispered, knocking gently.

The door opened. Mama had been waiting for her. She glanced furtively up and down the street, then grabbed Fae's arm and pulled her inside, slamming the door behind her.

"Oh, Fae," she said. "I thought you might not come." Her arms encircled Fae, and her smell was still the same – a homecoming smell.

Fae was surprised. "Of course, I came," she said. "Where else would I go?"

Mama stepped back and stared at her, and Fae saw something break behind her eyes. Then she pulled herself together. "Come on," she said. "There's a pie in the oven. I'm sure you're hungry."

"Pie?" Fae gasped. She couldn't remember when last she'd eaten something hot and hearty that hadn't been stolen.

Mama headed deeper into the house, and Fae stayed close beside her. The house was so different to the way it had been when Fae had left. There were new paintings on the walls; one of them was of green hills and blue skies, and it made Fae long for the country. The kitchen was filled with the wonderful smell of the baking pie, and Mama pulled out a chair for her.

"Sit, darling," she said.

"I'm dirty, Mama," said Fae sheepishly, glancing from the clean chair to her filthy dress.

"That's all right. We can always clean," said Mama.

"Mama?"

The small voice came from the doorway. Fae and Mama both looked up to see Edith standing there, wringing her hands in her pretty little frock, staring at Fae with big eyes.

"Edith," said Fae, beaming. She held out her arms. "Come to me."

Edith backed away. "Who is she?" she asked Mama.

Fae stopped, shocked. "You don't remember?" she whispered breathlessly.

"Of course, she doesn't," said Mama gently. She went over to Edith and scooped her into her arms. "She was only a baby when I sent... when you left for the country." She gave Edith a kiss on the cheek. "This is your sister, Edith. This is Fae. She's going to be staying with us."

"My sister?" Edith's eyes widened. "Really?"

"Yes, really."

Edith stared at Fae, fear and doubt loud in her expression. Fae looked down, suddenly feeling less welcome in her own home than she had been out on the streets.

Maybe this wasn't going to be as easy as she'd hoped.

※

Edith's rocking horse had a long, flowing black mane and tail made of real horsehair. The hair bounced and bobbed as the horse rocked to and fro, Edith clinging to its reins and screaming with laughter as Fae pushed the horse to a greater pace.

"Giddy up!" cried Edith, laughing breathlessly. "Faster! Faster!"

"As you wish, Princess Edith!" laughed Fae, giving the horse an extra nudge. Its rockers juddered across the floor, and Edith howled in glee.

Mama looked up from her armchair, where she sat with her embroidery. "Now, now, you girls," she said, laughter bubbling under the service of the admonition. "Gently, or you're going to break it."

"All right, Mama," said Fae, letting the horse slow down.

Edith jumped down from the horse and ran over to Fae, wrapping her arms around Fae's knees and gazing up at her. She had such plump, rosy cheeks and bright eyes. Fae thought of Peggy, who had been hiding in the alley for the two weeks that Fae had been living with Mama. When she'd been there that morning to bring the children something to eat, the little girl's cheeks were pinched and pale, her eyes wide with fear, dull with exhaustion.

"I'm so glad you came back, Fae," said Edith.

Fae dragged her thoughts back to the present moment. "I'm glad I came back, too," she said, brushing a stray lock of hair out of Edith's eyes. "I missed you so much."

"I always thought I'd dreamed you up," said Edith. "I used to have dreams about playing with a big sister when I was a baby, but I thought it was all my imagination." She cuddled Fae closer. "But now you're here, and I was scared of you at first. I remember you now. I love you, Fae."

Fae smiled at Edith's childlike enthusiasm. "I love you too," she said, hugging the little girl.

"I can't wait to tell Papa all about you," said Edith.

"No!"

Mama's voice shattered the warm moment. She lunged to her

feet, her embroidery tumbling, forgotten, from her lap. Seizing Edith's arm, she dragged her away from Fae.

"Edith, you listen to me." Her hands were trembling as she grabbed Edith's shoulders and glared into her eyes. "You don't breathe a word about Fae to your papa, do you understand? Not a word. Not a single word."

Edith's eyes were filled with tears. "Why not, Mama?"

"Don't ask me questions!" Mama gave Edith a shake. Her face was so pale. "Just do as I say. You don't speak of Fae to your papa. Not at all. Do you understand?"

Tears running down her cheeks, Edith nodded, too frightened to speak. "Go to your room," Mama ordered.

Sobbing quietly, Edith ran out of the room. Fae backed away, nervous of her mother's wrath. "I'll hide quietly again when he comes this evening, Mama," she said. "I promise."

"You had better," said Mama, but her voice was filled with weariness now, all of her anger gone. "I'm going to speak to him tonight, Fae. But I warned you, and I'm warning you again. I don't know what he's going to say."

Fae nodded, trying not to think about the possibilities. "Thank you, Mama."

There was the sound of hoofbeats outside. Mama hurried to the window and pulled the curtain aside to peer into the street. She turned to Fae, her face blanching. "Go! Get into your hiding place."

Fae didn't need to be told twice. She hurried into Edith's room, ignoring her sister's look of panic, and stumbled into Edith's wardrobe. Mama closed the door softly on her, sealing her in the dusty darkness. The four walls pressing around her felt like a reassurance as Fae waited, holding her breath, listening. Mama's footsteps hurried out of the room, and there was a long silence. Then voices in the corridor. Geoffrey's voice rumbling something. She couldn't tell if he was angry or not.

The voices came closer. Mama was talking just outside Edith's door. "... in her room. She was being disobedient, but you know how she is." Her laugh sounded strange. "Always so loud and playful."

"She meant no harm, I'm sure." Geoffrey's voice was surprisingly mellow.

Fae moved slightly so that she could put her eye to the crack in the great clock's door. Edith was sitting on her bed, quickly wiping away her tears. She straightened out her hair, tightened the bow in the end of her long braid and sat demurely on her bed, folding her hands in her lap.

The door opened, and Geoffrey came in. He was shorter than Fae remembered, and there were streaks of gray in his hair. Even his eyes were different; there was a softness to them now that Fae hadn't seen before.

"Hello, my little lamb," he said, smiling as he saw Edith.

"Papa!" Edith jumped off the bed and ran dutifully to him, holding out her arms.

Geoffrey picked her up and lifted her onto his hip, beaming at her. "I hear you've been a naughty little girl," he said.

Edith cast her eyes to the floor. "I'm sorry, Papa."

"Don't worry. I was a naughty little boy, too." He glanced around the room, and Fae thought she saw regret in his eyes. "A naughty young man, too, if we're honest." He kissed her forehead. "I know you didn't mean any harm. Come on. Let's go and play on that wonderful rocking horse of yours, what do you say?"

Edith's face lit up. "Yes, Papa, yes!"

Geoffrey put her down, and she ran out into the corridor. His laugh boomed as he followed her. Mama held the door, and once they were both out of the room, she gave a nervous glance toward the wardrobe, but didn't say a word to Fae. She closed the door behind her.

Fae sat in the dark and squeezed her eyes shut, praying with all of her might. Geoffrey seemed so different, so much older and gentler. She knew he was going to tell Mama she could stay.

She knew everything was going to be just fine.

Fae waited until Edith had been put to bed and her soft, deep breaths grew rhythmic and slow before slipping out of the wardrobe. Edith's face had the innocence and luminescence of a fallen moon on her pillow; she didn't stir as Fae tiptoed across the room to the door. She leaned against it, her ear to the doorway. Mama and Geoffrey were talking, but their voices were muffled. It sounded like they were in Mama's bedroom.

Slowly, so that the hinges wouldn't creak, Fae slipped the door open. She had sneaked around so much of London by now that it was second nature to make her way down the corridor and up to her mother's bedroom door without making the tiniest sound. She looked around, spotting a gap between a bookshelf and the wall for a hiding place in case Mama or Geoffrey came out of the room, then knelt down and put her ear to the door.

"She looks just like you, Belle." Geoffrey's voice was sonorous with affection. "Every day she grows more and more like you."

"On the contrary, I think Edith looks like you," said Mama. There was something stilted in her voice.

"She certainly has my spirit," said Geoffrey. "It's not easy to tell her what to do. But she will learn. You'll make a lady of her yet, my favorite secret." Fae heard him kiss Mama.

"Geoffrey..." Mama's voice was cautious. "There's something that I'd like to ask you."

"Anything for you, my beauty," murmured Geoffrey.

"It's about Fae."

There was a moment of silence. Fae held her breath. When Geoffrey spoke again, his voice was as low and dangerous as a snake. "What about her?"

"She's... she's back in London," said Mama slowly. "My parents are dead, Geoff. She had nowhere else to go."

"Surely you're not saying she's in this house?" demanded Geoffrey.

"No!" Mama's voice was frightened. "No, she's not here. She's – on the streets. I wouldn't let her come in without asking you, Geoff. You know that."

Fae squeezed her eyes shut. If Mama was lying about her, then she knew Geoffrey must look even angrier than he sounded.

"Good," said Geoffrey. "Because you know that the answer is no, Belle. She can't come here. There's no way that can ever happen again. The child is a nuisance. She's nothing but trouble – nothing like my sweet little Edith."

"But she has nowhere else to go, Geoff."

"Are you talking back to me, woman?" Geoffrey's voice rose as suddenly and terribly as a storm wave. "Do you dare to question me?"

"No! No, Geoffrey, I'm so sorry, I..."

"Shut up!" yelled Geoffrey. "You should have known better than to ask me. How dare you talk back to me? No, shut up! Don't say anything!" His footsteps sounded, hard and heavy on the floor. "I won't allow this!"

Fae heard him moving toward the door. Quick as a shadow in the face of lantern light, she fled across to the gap behind the bookshelf and tucked herself in there, not moving, barely breathing. It was just in time. The bedroom door slammed open, and Geoffrey stormed out, his face scarlet with rage. His coat was unbuttoned, his hair awry. He turned back toward the room and held out a menacing finger. "Speak that child's name in front of me again and you'll pay for what you've done, woman," he spat.

"Geoffrey, please," Mama was begging, sobbing, but Geoffrey didn't care. He turned on his heel and stormed out of the house.

Fae waited until she heard the front door slam shut and then the thunder of a horse's hooves galloping up the street and disappearing into the town. She crept out from her hiding place and slunk into the bedroom. Mama was lying in a tangle of sheets, sobbing quietly into her pillow.

"Mama?" Fae whispered.

Mama sat bolt upright. Her eyes were filled with tears and rage. She clutched the sheets to her chest, screaming.

"Get out of here, Fae!" she screamed. "Just get away from here! Get out of this house!"

Her words were like a hot poker being thrust into Fae's chest. She took a few stumbling steps closer. "No, Mama, please," she begged. "Don't throw me out. I don't have anywhere else to go."

"You can't stay here, Fae," spat Mama. "Geoffrey will do something terrible if he finds you."

"He won't find me," Fae pleaded. "I'll hide. You know how well I can hide. I'll be as quiet as a mouse, and he'll never, ever find me." Tears poured down her cheeks. "Mama, you can't throw me out. Please."

Mama stared at her. Her entire slender body was trembling, and finally, she collapsed back into her pillows.

"Fine," she croaked. "But it's not going to last. He will find you, Fae, and then you will regret staying here."

Fae wanted so much to climb up onto that bed and feel Mama's arms around her, snuggling her close. But something about the tone of Mama's voice drove her back out of the room. She slipped into Edith's room and curled up on the hearth rug, shocked into silence.

Mama's words chilled her to the very bone.

CHAPTER 10

For Fae, the next week and a half passed in a haze. There were moments with Edith that were pure joy; the little girl had fallen thoroughly in love with her sister, and there were times when they were playing together that Fae could almost forget about the looming specter of Geoffrey, who always seemed to be in the back of her mind.

Mama was kind. She drew Fae warm baths and bought her a brand-new dress that smelled wonderful – Fae didn't think she'd ever had a dress that hadn't belonged to somebody else first. As for her cooking, it was everything that Fae had dreamed of on those long, lonely, hungry nights lost in London. There was always enough that she could slip out after dark and bring a few scraps to Peggy and Lucas every night. She prayed that Mama wouldn't notice.

The night air was cool as Fae slipped out of the scullery window, her slim frame fitting easily through the little window. She kept a few scones, wrapped delicately in a clean napkin, close to her chest as she hurried along the street toward the alleyway where Peggy and Lucas were waiting for her. The scones were warm against her skin, and she hoped they would fill their hungry little bellies.

The flicker of firelight inside the alley was a warm reassurance. There was a part of Fae that worried every night that the children might not be there – that they'd just be gone somehow, just like Ollie and Grandma and Grandpa. But they weren't gone. They were huddled together underneath their tattered blanket, and when Fae came around the corner and into the alleyway, they lunged to their feet and ran toward her.

"Fae!" cried Peggy, grabbing Fae's soft, new skirt in her dirty hands. "I'm so glad you came."

"I come every night, dear," said Fae, bending down to kiss the top of Peggy's head. Her heart squeezed with pity as she gazed down at the little girl's lousy, matted hair. What was it about the world that made it so that Edith, just a few hundred yards away, was at this moment in a warm bath of soapy water, splashing and playing with her toys with a full belly – while sweet little Peggy was huddled in an alleyway with two sticks of firewood and just one cooling scone to eat all day?

Lucas didn't say anything. He just wrapped his arms around

Fae's legs and buried his face in her skirt. Fae stroked the top of his head.

"Come on," she said. "I've got scones for you. They're still nice and hot – and buttery. You'll love them."

"Scones," murmured Lucas, looking up. His eyes widened as he spotted the napkin in Fae's hand.

"Sit down," Fae instructed, bundling the children back up in their blanket beside the little fire. "Here you are. Eat them quickly while they're still hot – they'll warm you up." She gave each of them a scone and watched as they tore them ravenously into bits and devoured them. "I'm sorry I couldn't bring more."

"When can we come and live with you, Fae?" asked Peggy.

Fae swallowed, remembering Mama's confrontation with Geoffrey.

"Soon," she lied, not knowing what else to say. "As soon as I can come and get you, I will. Don't worry." She tried to smile, hoping to convince herself as well as the children. "Everything is going to be all right."

Her scone finished, Peggy sighed, tucking the blanket more tightly around herself and leaning her head on Lucas' shoulder. "At least we get nice food here, I guess," she said. "And nobody bothers us here. There's no angry drunk men or anyone trying to hurt us."

"That's right, Peggy," said Fae. "And you won't have to stay in this alley much longer." She prayed the words were true. "Soon, you'll get to come home with me."

It was always a wrench to leave the children behind and head back toward the warm home where Fae knew she would be sleeping soundly and in a safe room. What was she going to do now? She knew she couldn't convince Geoffrey to let Peggy and Lucas come to the house, not if he'd reacted so violently just to the mention of her name. Maybe she should just leave and take the children back to a place where they could pick pockets for a living again and hide out in a warehouse or an alley. Fae chewed her lip, the thought filling her with dread. She'd spent such a long time searching for her mama. She couldn't bear to walk away from her again now.

She'd already lost too many of the people she loved.

Reaching the scullery window, Fae climbed up onto an upturned old bucket she'd found in the alleyway and pulled herself through the window. Quietly, she slipped to the floor. With any luck, Mama was still bathing Edith and getting her dressed for bed and hadn't even missed her. She pushed open the scullery door, walked into the kitchen and found herself face-to-face with Geoffrey.

He was standing by the kitchen table, lounging against one of the chairs as Mama stood washing the dishes, and when Fae walked in, he looked up. There was no time to flee. His sharp eyes locked onto her at once, and Fae froze, knowing she was trapped.

The silence trembled with tension. The only sound Fae could hear was her own heart thundering in her ears.

"Belle." Geoffrey's voice had a flatness to it that was far more terrifying than any scream of rage could have been. "Who is this?"

Mama looked up, and her face drained of color. Fae took a step backwards. "Geoff..." Mama began.

"It can't be your older child," said Geoffrey, his voice still frighteningly calm. "Even though it looks just like her, I know it can't be, because I expressly ordered you not to ever let that child set her grubby feet in my house again."

Mama swallowed visibly. "I can explain."

Geoffrey whirled around, the movement so sharp and sudden that it made Fae jump. "What exactly can you explain, woman?" he shrieked, the sound resounding through the house. "Can you explain that you have disobeyed me? Can you explain that you have disrespected me after I gave you everything that you could ever have wanted?"

Tears were pouring down Mama's cheeks. "Geoffrey, I'm sorry, I'm so, so sorry. Please..."

Geoffrey drew back his hand. His slap rang across Mama's face, knocking her to her knees.

"Mama!" Fae cried out.

Mama raised a soapy hand to her reddening cheek, looking up at Geoffrey, terror written large on her face. Geoffrey leaned down and plucked Mama to her feet by the front of her bodice.

"I have slaved away to give you everything you need, you foolish cow," he spat in her face. "I gave you a house. I gave you a daughter. I even gave you secrecy so that my wife would never find out about you. For years, I've cared for you and kept you, ever since pulling you out of that brothel. And this is how you would treat me?"

He shook her so hard that her head whipped back and forth; he was screaming now, his nose inches from her face. "By lying to me and disobeying me?"

Mama didn't say anything. She just sobbed, a small and hopeless sound that would go unheeded. The sound ripped at Fae's heart, and she stepped forward, her voice sounding strange and frantic to her own ears.

"Let my mama go!"

Geoffrey tossed Mama down. She fell to the floor, and he wheeled around to face Fae, his face scarlet, eyes popping.

"You!" he snarled, storming toward her, his hands outstretched to grab her. Terror seized Fae's heart, and she stumbled back, her back slamming against the wall. Before she could move, Geoffrey had grabbed her arm, his hand closing like a ruthless vice. He drew back his free hand, bunching it into a fist, and Fae could see in his eyes how forceful the blow was going to be. She cringed back, her eyes closed, fear pounding through her entire body—

"Geoffrey, no!" Mama screamed.

Geoffrey's hand relaxed on Fae's arm for just an instant. An instant was all she needed. She twisted, wrenching her arm out of his grip, and bolted. He roared in anger, the sound spurring Fae to run faster. She crashed through the scullery, knocking jars and tins from the shelves in her panicked flight.

"Come back here!" Geoffrey bellowed.

But Fae had reached the window. She grabbed the sill, pulling herself up through the welcome gap and into the cool night. Geoffrey's hand closed on her ankle, and she kicked out desperately with her other foot. She felt an impact, and he cried out in pain and rage, pulling his hand away.

Fae tumbled through the window, landing heavily on her left shoulder. She didn't have time for the pang of pain that shot through it. Scrambling to her feet, she looked down the long and lamp-lit street, knowing she would never outrun him. Her eyes rested on a large garbage can nearby. She ran to it, pulled open the lid, and flung herself inside, pulling the lid back over her.

For a few terrible minutes, she listened as Geoffrey's footsteps stormed up and down the street looking for her. He was shouting, screaming like one possessed, his rage let loose like some angry red spirit that painted the night sky with the sound of blood. But he didn't find her. Instead, he went back into the house. And it wasn't long before Fae heard the sound of fists meeting flesh. And with each blow, the renewed cries of her mama, sobbing.

Fae knew Geoffrey was beating Mama because of her. It had happened again – that thing that was so wrong with her, that caused so much pain and grief to everyone around her. It was what had made Geoffrey pick up little Edith by her arm when she was just a baby. It had killed Grandma and Grandpa, driven Ollie out of her life, and gotten Rosa arrested. And now, its latest victim was the person Fae loved most in the world – her mother.

The garbage around her squelched, releasing an awful stench, as she quietly slipped back out of the garbage can and closed it behind her. Her mother's sobs still filled the night as Fae trudged down the street, heading back toward the alleyway. She only had two people left in the world – Peggy and Lucas. And how long would it be before the same thing happened to them?

As it turned out, it wouldn't be long. When Fae reached the alleyway, there was nothing. There was no blanket, no scraps of food, no fire, and no children. For a moment, confused, Fae looked up and down the street. Was this the wrong alley? She took a step forward, squinting into the shadows, and her foot bumped against something that broke at the touch. Looking down, Fae saw two charred little sticks and a heap of ash. When she knelt down and touched the ash, it was as ice cold as if it had never burned.

Fear jolted through Fae's heart. She straightened, her breath racing, body trembling as tears began to gather in her cheeks. Where had they gone? What had happened to them?

"Peggy!" she screamed, heedless of the danger of revealing herself, running out into the street. "Lucas! Where are you?"

Her cry echoed down the empty street, but there was no response. She started to run, not knowing which direction to go in, just knowing that she had to find them. "Peggy!" she shrieked. "Lucas! Peggy! LUCAS!"

She ran until her legs would no longer carry her. She screamed until her voice had been beaten into a reddened, raw pulp and slunk away, leaving her silent and breathless, cowering under the sparse shelter of a footbridge somewhere in the great, empty, loveless labyrinth of London. And there, crying voicelessly, she sobbed until she ran out of everything – hope, tears, energy – and drifted into something that could have been sleep. But it felt like death.

OLLIE STARTLED AWAKE. HE SAT UP, TANGLED IN SWEATY sheets, puffs of steam curling in the air from his hot, frantic breaths. His pulse pounded as he looked around the room, but there was nothing different here; just his single bed and the starlight drifting in from the window. It must be near to midnight.

Letting out a gentle groan, Ollie leaned back against his pillows again, allowing the air to softly cool his sweaty brow. It had been a long day of haymaking, and tomorrow promised more of the same; his joints and muscles still ached, and his scratchy eyes cried out for sleep. Yet his stuttering heart wouldn't stop hammering. Sitting up, Ollie climbed out of bed and walked over to the window. He opened it, relishing the cold air, and leaned his elbows on the windowsill.

The oak stood in the garden like a giant, solemn monument to a time that Ollie still missed with all his heart. He closed his eyes, remembering the hundreds of games of tag he'd played with Fae beneath those branches. *Fae.* The image of her face in his mind sent a stab of fear down his spine. He opened his eyes wide, staring out at the night. That was what his dream had been about. She'd been screaming his name over and over, and she'd been in some kind of danger – he couldn't quite make out what, but there seemed to be violence around her. Like a fire, or a storm at sea. Either way, he remembered her eyes with crystal clarity. The terror in them had screamed into his very soul.

It had felt so real. Ollie ran a hand through his damp hair, trying to calm himself, but he couldn't shake the feeling that something was wrong – very wrong. He didn't know what. He didn't even know if Fae was still alive, or if perhaps he really had dreamed her up like Otis and his parents thought.

"No," Ollie said aloud, the soft word curling on a cloud of steam. He knew she was real, just as real as the branches of the oak tree in front of him. Ever since he and Otis had moved here to manage the farm, Ollie had stared at that tree every day, knowing it was a silent testimony to the girl who had once lived there. He knew she'd been here, and he also knew that she was in trouble.

Knowing that she was in danger, but not knowing where she was, was like having both his hands cut off. He allowed his legs to give way under him, sliding down until his knees hit the dirt. Hands interlocked above his head, he leaned his forehead against the wall and did the only thing he could think of doing for her.

He began to pray.

Fae couldn't tell if she was hungry anymore. It had been so long since her stomach had known any kind of sustenance that it seemed to have simply stopped working entirely, as if it had simply disappeared out of her body. She knew she was cold, though. Wrapping her arms around her body, she staggered down the dark and lonely street, staring down at her feet as they somehow managed to keep going on the pavement. Both of her shoes had given out at the toe somewhere in the time since she'd left Mama's house – she couldn't tell if it had been days or weeks or maybe an eternity.

Now, with every step she took, she could catch a glimpse of her bare, pink flesh. She remembered that Amy, one of the street children, only had three toes on her right foot and two on the left. Amy said that the other toes had frozen and dropped off in the awful winter before she'd found Rosa and the gang. Fae wondered idly if her toes were going to fall off, too.

The first few nights had been nothing but panic. Running from street to street, crying out for Peggy and Lucas. She slept only when she could no longer run, and even that sleep was filled with nightmares of Geoffrey and the children. Fae wasn't sure how long it had taken before she'd come to terms with the awful truth: just like Ollie, Peggy and Lucas were never going to respond to her cries.

She truly was alone this time. There was no friendly gypsy or spotted horse named Samson, no fiercely kind Rosa to save her now. She still wore the gypsy's crystal on the string around her neck, but even its hope and magic seemed to have rubbed off.

A burst of music and laughter from an open window caught Fae's attention. She stopped, gazing disinterestedly up at the big house beside her. Somehow, she'd found her way into a posh uptown district, where the mansions of rich families lined every street. There must be a party inside this one. Brilliant candlelight filled the big window just above her head, and she caught glimpses of laughing men with champagne glasses, women with their hair done up in lovely curls and held in place with bejeweled pins that looked like scattered stars. Fae sighed. She'd tried going up to the servants' entrances of some of these places, knocking on doors and asking for work, but she usually got a slap or a kick in reply.

One kindly housekeeper, though, had given her a crust of bread. Maybe she'd be lucky this time, too. She shuffled back into motion, heading around to the back of the house and stumbling up the dark little path to the servants' entrance. It seemed like it took the last of her strength to knock on the door.

There was no response. Fae waited, staring at nothing. There were busy, kitchen sounds coming from inside – something sizzling on a stove, pot lids clanging, voices and feet hurrying to and fro. Frowning, Fae realized she'd been waiting a few minutes. Maybe they hadn't heard her. She raised her hand and knocked again.

The door opened, and a flood of warmth and light washed over Fae, momentarily taking her breath away. The housekeeper stood in the doorway, a plump figure with graying hair caught up in a bun, surrounded by the delicious aroma of something cooking.

"Good evening, ma'am—" Fae began.

"Are you looking for work?" demanded the housekeeper.

Startled, Fae stopped, staring up at her.

"Well, are you, or aren't you?" the housekeeper snapped.

"Y-y-yes," stammered Fae.

"What are you waiting for?" The housekeeper pulled the door wider. "Get in here. We were short-staffed as it is, and then poor Maisie went off with the angels last night, and now it's the master's big party, and he just won't stop shouting for things."

Fae hesitantly stepped into the warm kitchen. It was filled with a flurry of activity; no one even paused to look at her as maids in impeccable uniforms rushed this way and that, a row of sweating cooks scurrying and swearing by the stoves.

"Come on!" said the housekeeper, looking her up and down. "You're a little grubby, but you'll do all right after a quick scrub. We've got to hurry. They want the main course out there in twenty minutes."

Before Fae could say anything, she was whisked into the servant's quarters, and the housekeeper was shouting at a handful of petrified scullery-maids who half-filled a tin bath with tepid water in record time.

"Bathe quickly," said the housekeeper, dumping a pile of unfolded clothes on a chair beside the bath. "Try to get the worst of the knots out of your hair and get into these clothes. You're a little smaller than Maisie was, but you'll have to do."

Fae looked from the bath to the clothes to the housekeeper in mute astonishment. Was this really happening? Had she really found work?

"Now, girl!" snapped the housekeeper.

"Yes, ma'am," Fae started pulling her dress over her head as the housekeeper and maids rushed out of the room. She sank into the bathwater, relishing the feeling of the clean water on her skin, even though it was rather lukewarm. Pausing for a moment, Fae tried to collect her thoughts. If what the housekeeper said was true, then the clothes lying on that chair had been taken from a poor dead girl's body. Fae wasn't sure she liked the idea.

Still, she definitely liked the idea of being somewhere safe and warm tonight, with something to eat and a place to sleep. Poor dead Maisie didn't need that anymore, but Fae certainly did. A sense of hope started to dawn on her, a feeling of being given a second chance.

She had to make the most of it. She grabbed the hard, little bar of soap from the ground beside the bath and began, determinedly, to scrub.

PART III

CHAPTER 11

Four Years Later

"Fae! Fae! You're late!"

The sharp voice dragged Fae from the depths of her sleep. She stirred, feeling the walls of the cupboard pressing against her back and shoulders. There wasn't enough room inside to stretch, so she just raised her head, muffling a yawn. Maybe she had imagined the voice. Perhaps she could go back to sleep, just for five more minutes.

"FAE! Where is that cursed girl?" shouted the housekeeper's voice nearby.

So, she hadn't imagined it. Fae put her feet down, slipping off the pile of boxes she'd been sleeping on, and laid a hand against the cupboard door in front of her. She lingered for a second, enjoying one more moment of darkness. She knew she was about to start another long day of being shouted at and pushed around, but at least there would be a meal and a place to sleep at the end of it.

"Fae!" bellowed the housekeeper.

Fae pushed open the door and stepped out of the cupboard. The housekeeper, who was only a few feet away, jumped a mile.

"What on earth?" she cried, her eyes popping. "What were you doing in there, you stupid girl? You've got a bed in the same room as the other girls, don't you?"

"It's quieter in there," said Fae. She couldn't tell the housekeeper the truth: that the further she kept herself from others, the better. Hiding alone was the only way that she – and those around her – would be safe.

The housekeeper shook her head. "Touched, you are," she said. "And late. Get yourself into that kitchen. Now!"

Fae scurried demurely into the kitchen. The cook had not come in yet, but a bunch of kitchen and scullery maids were hurrying around, lighting the fires and preparing for another long day in the manor.

"Oh, there she is," snapped one of the maids, spotting Fae. "Was the usual hour too early for you, your highness?" Her voice dripped with sarcasm.

"She thinks she's all special because she's been made a parlor maid," said another. "Would you like us to serve your tea in bed, your majesty?"

"She doesn't sleep in a bed," laughed the first. She tapped her forehead. "Mad as a hatter."

Fae made no comment. It was best not to speak to the others, she'd found; it was best not to speak to anyone, but to remain invisible. She gathered up her basket of cleaning things and headed up the stairs into the rest of the house.

She could only assume that she'd been made a parlor maid because of her skill of invisibility. Slipping like a shadow from room to room, she made sure that first the dining room and then the master's study were spotless, every surface clean and polished to a fine shine. The work was lonely and mindless, and that suited Fae just fine. For four years, the only people she saw for most of the day was the master's family, and they seemed to look straight through her. As if she were nothing but a stray breeze.

Everyone except for the master, that was. Lately, she'd noticed him spotting her more and more often. She didn't know what the look in his eyes really meant, but she didn't want to find out, either. She hurried to finish cleaning his study so that it would be ready for him by the time he'd finished breakfast, then took the long way around to the bedrooms, avoiding the staircases that he would take from the dining room to his study.

The hallways were silent and empty as Fae padded down them toward the master bedroom, her basket cradled safely on her arm. She ignored the imposing stares of the portraits on the walls, reached the gilded door of the master bedroom, and pushed it open.

The canopy bed was vast and unmade, its luxurious silk draperies making Fae long for sleep. She put her basket down on the armchair by the fireplace and picked up a duster, turning to the ornaments on the mantelpiece. Humming softly to herself, she started to work the duster over the staring face of a marble bust on the end of the mantelpiece.

"Finally." The masculine voice came from somewhere behind her. "I've caught you."

Fae's hand jerked, sending a little china dog plummeting from the mantelpiece. It shattered on the hearth, and she spun around, her feet crunching in the china. Her heart hammered as she stared toward the bed. The master sat up, pushing his covers back. There was something predatory in his eyes as he stared at her.

"You've been avoiding me," he said.

Fae swallowed hard. She grabbed her basket, hugging it close to her body. "I – I'm sorry, sir. I wasn't aware that you were still in bed." She glanced toward the door; she would have to pass the bed to reach it. "I won't disturb you further."

Fae moved toward the door, but the master got up and

stepped into her path. He was wearing only his long white night-robe, and Fae averted her eyes, trembling with fear and shame. She heard the door close, then the master's footsteps as he came closer to her.

"You know, I don't even recall when you became part of our staff," he said, his voice low and prowling. "I don't think I noticed you then. You were nothing but a little scrap of a thing." His fingertips found her arm, lifting it, his big hands moving over her fingers. "You've rather blossomed in the last few years."

Fae took a step back and felt the pressure of the mantelpiece behind her. She didn't dare to lift her eyes. "I have to go, sir," she whispered.

"Not yet," said the master. He stepped closer to her, the heat of his body invading her skin. His fingertips traced up her arm, finding her shoulder, her neck, her jaw. They pressed lightly under her chin, forcing her to look up. His eyes were glowing coals, and the most frightening thing that Fae had ever seen.

"Such a beauty," he murmured, his thumb stroking her chin. He leaned closed to her, his lips moving inches from hers, his breath hot on her face as he spoke. "Such unwitting beauty."

Fae pulled her head back, craning her neck as far as she could. "Please, sir," she whimpered. "Let me go."

"Why so frightened, you pretty little thing?" The master

caressed her cheek with the back of her hand, a dangerous smile playing on his lips. "You have nothing to fear. I'll be good to you. I'll give you everything you need, and no one will ever know." He was closer to her again now, the length of his body trapping her against the fireplace. "You'll be my secret."

Secret. My favorite secret. Geoffrey's words came crashing back to Fae, and she closed her eyes as the master leaned closer; seeing her mother's life. Her mother's imprisonment in that house. Hearing her sobs as Geoffrey's fists pounded into her. The master's lips met hers, and fear and determination rushed through her like an uncontrolled fire. She couldn't have that life. She would *not* have that life.

She flailed, wanting to scream, but his mouth was over hers, trapping the scream inside and throwing it back into her heart to boil there. Her desperate fingers found a hard surface beside her right shoulder, something hard and round. The neck of the bust. Her hand closed on it, and she used all of her strength to bring it around toward the master's head.

There was an awful crack. The pressure of the master's lips disappeared suddenly, replaced with a yelp of pain. He took a staggering step back, and Fae breathed in a great gasp of relief, feeling as if she could taste the air again for the first time since he rose from the bed. The master raised a hand to his head in her blurred vision, anger and disbelief mingling on his face. He lowered his hand, and there was blood on his fingers, blood in his hair, blood trickling down his forehead.

His knees buckled, and he fell to the floor with a meaty thump.

A gasp of horror ripped from Fae's lips. The bust fell from her fingers and landed on the floor with a crack. She stared down at the master's limp body, blood spreading into his hair.

"I've killed him," she croaked, her hands raised to her lips. They felt bruised from his hateful kiss. "I've killed him."

There was shouting from elsewhere in the house, but Fae couldn't look up from the master's body until she saw it: his chest rising. His limp hand twitched, and his fingers curled into a fist. He wasn't dead, but he was definitely about to be very angry, and there were footsteps coming up the hallway toward her.

Fae didn't think. She just dove into the fireplace, looked up into the inviting darkness of the chimney, and began to climb. It was almost too narrow to admit her shoulders, but she squashed them in somehow, pulling her skirts out of view just as the door of the bedroom opened. Running feet came into the room, and Fae held her breath, feeling soot tumbling into the folds of her dress. Her knees were pressed up against one side of the chimney, her back against the other. For the first time, she was thankful for the long hours she spent scrubbing the floors. Her muscles trembled but did not tire as angry voices shouted in the bedroom. One of them was the master's.

"Find her!" he shouted. "Find her and string her up! She tried to kill me!"

The feet hurried back out of the bedroom. And Fae did the only thing she knew how to do: she stayed hidden.

It was only when the room had been silent for several minutes that Fae finally climbed down out of the fireplace and into the empty room. There was still a bloodstain on the floor where the master had been lying; the nose of the bust was cracked, and her basket lay on the floor, its contents scattered everywhere. Her heart was fluttering like a broken-winged bird. She would have to get out of here. If they found her, she had no doubt that she would be hanged.

On her left, the bay window where the mistress liked to sit and read was invitingly open. Fae took off her shoes, holding them in one hand as she padded toward it, leaving a trail of soot on the floor. It opened soundlessly at her push. There was a great oak tree standing right beside the window, and grasping its branches felt like second nature. Fae thanked Ollie in her thoughts as she climbed onto one of its boughs and moved silently through the canopy until she could drop down onto the wall at the end of the garden and, from there, climb onto the street and disappear into the crush of people heading to work in the summer sunshine.

The crowd was far too busy to notice one shabby little parlormaid covered in soot. She moved with them until she reached a busy marketplace, then slipped into the shadows and hid in an abandoned doorway, catching her breath and staring out at the buzzing crowd that filled the little square.

What was she going to do next? She was alone. No one from the manor house would ever help her; Peggy and Lucas were long gone, despite the many nights she'd escaped from the manor and called their names in the streets until her voice grew hoarse. Mama was better off without her. Rosa, for all she knew, had been hanged for stealing. As for Grandma and Grandpa, they were long since gone.

The strength seemed to leave her body. She sank to the ground, her back to the doorway, and gazed dully at the bustling streets. She'd been in this city for six long years — six years of heartache and hardship, first scrounging on the streets, then suffering with Mama and Geoffrey, and then four years of abuse in the manor house. The stench of the city filled her nostrils, and something just as dark and insidious rose in her heart. It was hatred. Hatred for these streets, these grim-faced people, for the buildings that always hid the sky and the smoke that kept its beauty behind a pungent veil. Nothing good had ever happened to her underneath London's little scraps of polluted sky. She closed her eyes, trying to remember a time that she had ever been happy.

It came to her at once. A market morning in the winter, lying beneath the branches of the old oak tree, staring up at the sunlight where it shone between the bare twigs, just a few hours before Fae's world had fallen apart. She took a deep breath. She could almost feel the crispness of the snow on her back, the warmth of the sun on her face.

It's all about a man who gets stuck on an island all by himself. Ollie's voice was crystal-clear in her memory; she could see the glint in his eyes, the smile on his face. *He has to do all kinds of things to stay alive.*

"It's very exciting," Fae whispered, remembering. She felt just like Robinson Crusoe; stuck in a great city all by herself, even though she was surrounded by people. She felt alone and stranded. Thinking back to all the stealing and lying she'd had to do, she realized that just like Crusoe, she'd done whatever it took to survive.

She wondered how the story ended. She wondered if Crusoe ever got to go home and be safe and loved again, or if there was a home for him at all when he got back, or if he stayed on that island forever and eventually starved to death, old and alone.

She didn't want to find out what that felt like. She wanted to feel the sun on her face again and see the big, open sky of the country, the only place where she'd ever really been happy. In her mind's eye, she saw Ollie pushing his spectacles further up the bridge of his nose. *I think reading is more interesting than hitting each other and wrestling.*

I think you're interesting, Fae had said.

Interesting? Ollie's smile had lit up her entire world, split open her sky and filled it with angels and thunder. *And I think you're fascinating, so there.*

"Fascinating." It was the last time Fae had seen Ollie. She sat up, looking out at the marketplace, a plan forming in her mind. "He thinks I'm fascinating." She got to her feet, squaring her shoulders, feeling something roar deep in her belly or her soul. There was only one person who had ever been sunshine in her dark room, and he hadn't been there for her when she'd needed him the day her grandparents died, but maybe that hadn't been his fault. Maybe he was still out there in the country.

At any rate, anything was better than this smoky, smoggy, smelly city she hated so much.

Moving into the crowd, Fae made no more sound than a shadow. It had been four years since she'd last stolen anything, but when she brushed up against the young man who was running to hail a cab, it was second nature to swipe his pocket-watch before he even noticed. She spotted a pawn shop on the other side of the marketplace and made a beeline for it, the watch clutched in her hand, pushing aside the pang of regret that threatened as she felt its smooth shape in her hand. She didn't have any other choice.

Ten minutes later, the watch was gone, and a few shiny coins in its place; ten minutes after that and she was wearing a new dress and walking toward the train station with big, strong strides, ready for another life.

Ready to go home.

※

SUMMER HAD COME TO THE FARM THAT OLLIE AND OTIS had been running ever since the old Carter couple had passed away, and the hay fields were knee-deep in waving swathes of grass so green that staring at it for too long made Ollie's eyes hurt. He swung his feet over the gently stirring blades, sitting on the edge of the wagon, not caring that it smelled strongly of the manure they'd just finished shoveling onto the field for fertilizer. He took another bite out of the plowman's pie in the brown paper bag on his lap and stared at the fields in deep contentment.

"It's going to be a good first cutting," said Otis, beside him.

"And we'll be able to harvest it soon," Ollie agreed. "Maybe we'll get a third cutting in this year, too, if the rain stays good to us."

"I think so," said Otis. He grinned. "This little place sure has come a long way since you and I started working on it together. Old Mr. Carter had really neglected it, but now it's starting to live up to its full potential."

"Thanks to all your hard work," said Ollie, smiling. "You were so excited when Mama and Papa told you that it would be yours as soon as you turned eighteen. In the four years since, you've put your heart and soul into this place."

"Not so bad yourself, Ollie," said Otis, slapping his brother on the back. "I know you'd far rather read than make hay, but you've also been a great help, even though you were just a fourteen-year-old kid when we started."

"I can always read after making hay," said Ollie, with a wink.

"I just hope that soon we'll have someone to share this farm with," said Otis. His voice was uncharacteristically wistful, and Ollie gave him a questioning look. "What do you mean?"

"Oh, you know." Otis shrugged nonchalantly, but there was a scarlet bloom on his cheeks. "It would be nice to have – you know, wives."

Ollie laughed. "Does this have something to do with that pretty little brunette at market day?"

"Brunette? I don't know what you're talking about," protested Otis, but his blush deepened.

"I think you do," said Ollie, giggling. "The one with the sweet smile and the dark blue eyes that you stared into so deeply while I was trying to buy cheese from her."

"Nonsense," said Otis. "I was just – um – I was just lost in thought."

"Thoughts of her, no doubt," said Ollie. He gave his brother a good-natured shove. "Go on, admit it. You like her. And I know you've been seeing her in the evenings when you head out to 'have a pint with your friends'."

"Oh, all right! You're awful," said Otis, laughing. "Yes, I've been to see Myrtle a few times in the last few weeks. Her papa is a terrifying old goat, but he lets me in, and we go for walks in their garden and..." Otis gave a lovesick sigh. "She's so kind, Ollie. She just makes the world a better place simply by breathing."

"I knew it." Ollie grinned. "I'm happy for you, brother. You've been lonely. Also, you're just a dreadful cook."

"I am not."

"Yes, you are," said Ollie.

"I make a good bowl of porridge."

"That's true, but we can't eat porridge for breakfast, lunch and supper, Otis."

Otis relented. "Fair enough." He grinned widely. "Hopefully, soon, Myrtle will be standing in the kitchen when we get home from the hay fields."

"I hope so, too," said Ollie. "You deserve it."

There were a few moments of silence as the brothers chewed their pies, admiring the breathtaking rise of the green hill where it ran up to meet the house where they'd been staying for a few years. The oak tree topped it like the peak of a tiara.

"What about you?" said Otis.

"Me?" Ollie was puzzled.

"Yes, you. When are you going to start seeing a girl?" asked Otis. "Or are you still hung up on your imaginary girl from six years ago?"

Ollie looked away. "Fae wasn't imaginary," he said.

"You always get so annoyed when I suggest it, Ollie, but you have to admit it's a little strange," said Otis gently. "No one's ever heard of her, and if you ask anyone in the village, they don't know that Mrs. Carter ever had a granddaughter."

"She was a secret," said Ollie softly. "She said that I had to keep her a secret." He looked up at Otis, his heart hurting. "She was real, Otis, and she was my best friend. I know she was. We had such good times together."

"Real or not, Ollie, someday you're going to have to move on. You can't cling to her forever, because she's gone."

Ollie sighed. "I know you mean well, but I'm not going to let her go. For better or worse, whether she ever comes back or not, she's the only girl in the world who ever made my heart sing." He gazed into the distance, sadness settling over him. "And I'll continue to hope she'll find her way back to me, to the very last beat of my heart."

Otis sighed, draping a brotherly arm over Ollie's shoulders. "Let's hope it doesn't come to that."

"Let's hope," echoed Ollie.

CHAPTER 12

Part of Fae had been so frightened that her grandparents' house had never existed. That it had all been part of some wild dream she'd had as a child, where she'd imagined a world that didn't have four brick walls, a world with green grass and flowing hills and a sky so big it threatened to swallow up every puny human fear in its majesty.

It had half-surprised her at the train station when the ticket seller had recognized the name of the town; part of her thought it could not possibly still be there. But she'd bought a ticket and climbed on the train and sat staring out of the window as grimy, ghastly London was left far behind, and the countryside grew bigger and bigger around her until at last, they reached the station where Grandpa and Grandma had fetched her when she was just a little girl.

She wasn't a little girl anymore. The glances of the young men on the train as she'd made her way onto the platform said as much; she hadn't kept track of her birthdays, but she knew she had to be at least sixteen by now. Stepping onto the platform, though, she felt six again. Six and scared, and this time, there would be no grandparents to come and find her.

So she found herself. She made her own way, by memory, even by asking a stranger; unlike strangers in London, he didn't cuff her or spit on her. Instead, when she asked for the way to the Carters' home, he just pointed.

"But if you're looking for the Carters, I'm afraid you won't get very far, miss," he'd said. "They've been dead these six years already."

Now she was standing in front of the house as dusk rose up from the cracks in the hills and filled the sky with the sound of crickets. Had it really been six years since she'd stood before this door? It looked so much the same. There was the crown of the oak tree standing behind the house, just the top of it visible above the roof; the window-frames and the door were still the same color, although she could see they'd been recently repainted. And there were lights in the window. Those lights were the only reason why she hadn't run inside.

She wasn't sure what she'd expected. She hadn't really expected the house still to be here, but to have people living in it was unfathomable. Who could it be? What were they doing in her grandparents' old house?

A silhouetted figure moved in the kitchen window, and she heard a deep voice talking. Another figure joined it, and they stood at the sink together. It sounded like they were washing dishes, chatting casually; both voices were masculine and utterly unfamiliar. Fae took a step forward. Perhaps she should knock at the door. Tell them she used to live here. Ask them if they knew a young man named Ollie. She realized that she didn't even know Ollie's surname, and fear froze her to the spot. What if they wanted to hurt her, like the master had that morning?

Then, one of the figures moved toward the door, and the last of Fae's courage left her. A crack of lamplight fell onto the garden path, but by the time it widened, and the young man stepped outside, Fae had already fled, disappearing into the welcome darkness of the barn. She could see the outline of unfamiliar horses in the stalls where only old George had once stood; they stomped and whinnied when she came inside, so she kept running until she reached the ladder that led to the hayloft. Quick as she could, she scrambled into the loft. It was silent and dark and dusty, empty but for a pile of last year's hay right at the end.

Fae stayed on her hands and knees, panting and listening. No one had followed her. Exhaustion was making her arms tremble, and she had run out of options. She crawled quietly across the loft's floor until she reached the hay, then fell into its dusty embrace and allowed her mind to tumble into sleep.

"Move over, you old oaf. Come on – that's it. Good boy."

The voice was so gentle that Fae didn't mind that it had woken her. Delicious sunshine was playing gently over her body; she didn't stir in the hay, comfortable and sleepy, not bothering to open her eyes. She just wanted to listen to that voice. It was accompanied by the soft swish of a brush on a horse's coat.

"That's better, isn't it? Now you're all clean and ready to get to work." A harness creaked, and there was the gentle slap of leather meeting a horse's hide. "Good boy. Stand, now. That's a good boy."

"Chatting to the horses again, are you?" came another voice. This one was also pleasant, and a little playful. "You do know they're not going to answer you back, don't you?"

"Aw, I think Copper likes my voice." The first voice had such a familiarity to it. Fae felt she could listen to it all day long. "Don't you, hey, Copper?"

"As long as you tell him to do his work properly today, I don't care." The second voice laughed. "Come on – let's get them hitched up to the wagon and get moving."

"All right. Come along, Copper. Let's get this day started."

Hoofbeats clopped out of the barn, and Fae knew that this

would be her chance to go down to the house and find something to eat. But first, lulled by the softness of that familiar voice, she would let the sunlight be kind to her for a few more minutes and get just a little more sleep.

***

It felt strange to be stealing food out of what had once been her own home.

When Fae had woken from her wonderful snooze in the loft, she could see the two young men and their wagon through the little window at the top of the loft. They were far off in the hay field, hard at work, and she knew they probably wouldn't be back for quite a while. It was the perfect opportunity to slip down the barn and head into the house.

They hadn't locked the door. Nobody locked the door in the country, Fae knew; Grandma and Grandpa certainly hadn't. Walking back into the house was slow and sticky, as if the very air was as thick as treacle with memories. She stood in the living room for a long, long time, staring at the armchair where Grandpa had always sat smoking his pipe and listening to Grandma in silence. She wondered where his grave was. She would have to ask Ollie, when she eventually found him.

The kitchen, too, was exactly the way she'd left it. There was a bowl of fruit on the table; she stopped to wash her hands at the sink before carefully rearranging the fruit so that no one would notice she'd taken an apple right from the bottom of the pile. Two loaves of bread waited in the bin, one of them already cut. Fae didn't have to search for the bread knife – she just cut herself a few slices, washed the knife and tucked it away.

The bread was soft and so fresh and smelled heavenly. She paused at the window to take a few bites, gazing out at the oak tree. It was the only thing in the country that didn't seem smaller than it had been when she'd last seen it. The tree seemed to have grown as much as she had.

Hoofbeats sounded in the front yard. Seized with panic, Fae almost dropped the bread. She tucked it all into the pockets of her dress and bolted for the back door. The hoofbeats were coming around the corner as she reached the barn door, and she knew she didn't have time to make it all the way into the loft before they would be upon her. Trying to crush the rising panic in her chest, Fae dove behind the cart that stood against the barn wall. She peered between the spokes of the wheels, praying that the young men hadn't seen her.

The men came around the corner, riding in the hay wagon, which was empty except for a couple of shovels lying in its bed. The one who was driving was taller and had broad shoulders and dimples that showed as he laughed; the other was looking down, his hat shadowing his face.

"I just can't help it!" the taller one was saying. "She makes me so happy. I could just explode!"

"Clearly," commented the other. He was the one with the

pleasant voice, the one that had sounded so familiar that morning. Sunlight flashed on his spectacles as he turned his head away from Fae, looking up at the taller one. "So, when do I get to meet this Myrtle that's captured my brother's heart?"

"Soon enough," replied the taller man. "I'll ask her family over to our house to dinner – just as soon as Mama can help, anyway."

"Mama definitely needs to help," laughed the pleasant-voiced man. He reached up to push his spectacles further up the bridge of his nose, and the little gesture froze Fae's heart.

His voice was so familiar. And he was tall and slender, and wore spectacles, and about the right age. But surely... surely it couldn't be...

The young man turned, jumping down off the wagon, and Fae saw his face for the first time. It was a face that sent sunshine straight into the bottom of her soul, because she knew that face. She had gazed into its smile so many times, so long ago, and it had always brought her nothing but joy.

"It can't be..." she murmured.

But one moment later, she knew that it was, as the taller man pulled up the brake and looked down at the man with the spectacles.

"You're right," he said. "Our cooking just isn't going to cut it, Ollie."

It *was* him. It was him. She had found Ollie, and he had been here all along, caring for her grandparents' farm and keeping it exactly the same as it had always been just as if he had known, as if he had always known that she was going to come back to this moment and launch out from behind the cart and run to him and throw herself into his arms and tell him how much she had missed him—

Only she didn't. Rooted to the spot, Fae just stared as Ollie started unhitching the horses from the wagon, chatting to his brother without a care in the world. Mama had looked careless too, when she'd come walking down Crawley Street, hand-in-hand with Edith. And Fae had run out to greet her, and it had ended with Mama sobbing in the night as Fae fled into the streets.

What if the same thing happened with Ollie? What if he didn't know her? Worst of all, what if he didn't even remember her? He wouldn't have waited, all these years. Perhaps he would have forgotten.

So Fae didn't move. She just watched as he led the horses into the stable, even though her whole heart seemed to leap out of her chest and follow him.

OLLIE TOOK A BITE OF HIS TOAST AND CHEWED AS HE pondered his brother's question. "You know, I do think you're right," he said. "There *were* six apples in that bowl yesterday. I remember taking them out of the box and putting them there. Are you sure you didn't eat one and forget about it?"

"No, I'm quite sure," said Otis, staring in puzzlement at the fruit bowl. "And did you cut yourself some bread yesterday afternoon?"

"No, not at all. Why?" asked Ollie.

"One of the loaves has been cut. Look," said Otis, taking it out of the bread bin. "And there were crumbs on the counter when we got back from the hay fields, even though I'm sure I wiped it down after breakfast."

"Yes, you're right," said Ollie. "That's strange. I wonder what's going on."

"Maybe it's some homeless person," suggested Otis. He shuddered. "I know we don't have many in town, but more and more of them have been coming up from the city to glean in our fields. I hate to think of some grubby street man coming into our house. We'd better lock the door tonight."

"I don't even know where the key is," admitted Ollie. "But you're probably right – we don't want any of the Carters' things being stolen."

Otis laughed. "What, in case your fairy girlfriend comes back? Maybe she's the one who's been stealing the food."

Ollie tossed a crust of toast at his brother. "Maybe it's Myrtle who's been sneaking in to watch you sleep."

"All right." Otis laughed, picking up the crust from the floor. "I won't tease you about your girl, and you don't tease me about mine – even though mine is the only real one."

Ollie decided to let it go. "You're right that it could be a tramp, though. Maybe I should check the loft before we head out this morning. We haven't been in there much now that it's summer, and it would be an ideal place for someone to hide."

"Good idea," said Otis. He took his plate to the sink. "I'm going to walk over to Mama's quickly and ask her if she'll come and cook sometime this week so that we can invite Myrtle over."

"See you later," said Ollie.

Otis headed out of the front door. Ollie finished his toast and then made his way toward the barn, wondering what he'd do if he found a homeless person in the loft. He didn't want a prospective thief around anymore than Otis did, but he'd always felt so sorry for the people he'd seen sleeping under bridges or in doorways. Maybe Papa would know what to do.

He climbed the ladder and pulled himself into the muted peace of the loft. Shafts of sunlight filtered into the loft through the single window, blurring as Ollie moved in front of it; dust motes danced in the sun, illuminating nothing but dust and hay. Although there was something a little strange about the hay. Ollie went closer, frowning as he spotted a hollow in the remnants of last year's hay. There was an apple core lying beside it. He went over to the hay and crouched down, seeing some breadcrumbs dusting the floor. Otis was right. Someone had been stealing from them.

Something shiny caught the corner of Ollie's eye. Looking up, he saw a piece of cloth caught on a nail in the wall just to his left. He pulled the cloth off and opened it in his hands, and to his surprise, it was soft and silky. Just like the fabric of a girl's dress. Without really knowing why, he raised the fabric to his nose and sniffed, and the scent brought a thousand memories flooding back. Running in the grass of the garden. Making snow angels. Climbing in the boughs of the great tree. The sparkle in her eyes as she looked over him. *I think you're interesting.* He felt a hot tear course down his cheek and stared at the scrap of cloth in disbelief. Surely, surely it couldn't be her...

A floorboard creaked behind him. Hardly daring to hope, Ollie turned, and she was standing right there. Not the ten-year-old girl he'd known six years ago, but a slender young woman, her torn dress draping along her elegant curves, her lips slightly parted in surprise, like two perfect pink petals unfurling in the sun. She was taller, her hair longer, matted and messy, sprinkled with hay. But her eyes were the same. They were exactly the same, and the light in them, the expression, made Ollie feel as though a great tidal wave had just washed over him. It left him cold and dizzy and breathless where he stood, frozen, simply staring.

He would have built a home and lived inside that one glorious moment forever if he could. But it passed, and a single word managed to make its way out of his mouth.

"Fae?"

He saw her Adam's apple bob as she swallowed, and even that tiny movement seemed to set off fireworks in his world.

"Ollie," she whispered.

He didn't know if he jumped or ran to her. He just knew that he was suddenly beside her, and he was pulling her into his arms, tucking her safely into every curve of his shaking body, tears pouring down his cheeks as after six years of hoping, doubting, believing, praying – six years of being ridiculed for his trust in her existence, six years of longing just to see her smile, six years of agonizing guilt over not having gone to the house earlier, six years of wishing he could have protected her – after six years of torture—finally, and blessedly, he held her in his arms at last.

CHAPTER 13

When Ollie's arms first closed around her, Fae was overwhelmed with shock. It had been such a long time since anyone touched her fondly that she had forgotten how it felt. Then his smell struck her; a free and homely smell, filled with sunshine and sweet summer hay, and it brought tears to her eyes.

He smelled like home. And his arms felt like home, even though she had never felt them in this way before. Her knees buckled, and she allowed him to catch her, slowly sinking to the ground, drawing her into his lap. His arms were trembling where they encircled her, and her head was neatly tucked beneath his chin. She felt surrounded, tucked in.

For the first time since her grandparents had died, Fae felt safe.

"Ollie." She realized that the name was tumbling from her lips over and over. "Oh, Ollie, Ollie, Ollie." Her arms were around his neck and she was clinging to him for dear life. "Ollie. Ollie, I can't believe it's you."

"Oh, Fae." Ollie hugged her closer. "I never stopped. I never, ever, ever stopped. I need you to know that. I didn't stop, Fae."

Fae drew back just a little so that she could tilt up her head and look him in the eye. His spectacles were slightly askew. "What do you mean?" she whispered.

"I never stopped," Ollie repeated. "I never stopped believing in you." He was crying, but he reached up and wiped away her tears with a gentle brush of his thumb. "I never stopped looking for you, Fae. Everyone said you weren't real, but I waited for you all these years. I searched for you everywhere I knew, and when I couldn't search anymore, then I started waiting. I knew you would come home. I believed you would come home to me." He pushed his spectacles straight again, his eyes shining with tears behind them. "I never stopped loving you, Fae."

The emotion in the loft was a wave, but Fae was riding it, feeling her own heart soar at Ollie's words. She didn't know whether to laugh or cry.

"I came home to find you, Ollie," she whispered. "Nothing else ever worked. Mama didn't want me, and everything just went wrong. And I..." She paused. "I knew I needed to come and find you."

"I'm so glad you came to find me." Ollie took her hands in both of his; they were trembling. "I've missed you so much."

"I thought..." Fae swallowed. "I thought you might have forgotten me."

He leaned forward. The kiss he placed on her forehead, gently, delicately, was in every way the opposite of the kiss the master had forced upon her a few days ago. It warmed her skin like sunlight.

"Never," Ollie whispered, gazing intensely into her eyes. Slowly, a wide grin blossomed over his face. He straightened up, pulling her softly to her feet, still gripping her hand. "Come on!" he said. "I must show you to everyone!"

"What?" said Fae.

"I must show everyone how wonderful you are." Ollie laughed and set off down the ladder. "Come on!"

The next thing Fae knew, he was running, and she was running beside him, half-afraid and half-laughing, holding her skirts in her free hand. They ran through the house, their footsteps ringing like children's on the floor, and onto the lane and then they were heading toward town.

Fae, breathless, saw the signposts leading that way and fear planted her feet like roots. She stopped, yanking her hand away. Ollie stumbled to a halt, turning back to face her.

"Fae?" His face was full of pained confusion.

"I'm sorry, Ollie." She looked around nervously. Had anyone seen her? "I... I just can't."

His eyes were wide. "What do you mean?" he asked, his voice as gentle as it was hurting.

"I can't go out there." Her voice shook. "Everyone will see me."

Ollie took a slow step nearer. "But Fae, I want everyone to see you."

"No. No!" Fae backed away. "I can't do this, Ollie. Every time I stop hiding, bad things happen." Her eyes smarted with tears. "Mrs. Willows saw me and then Grandma and Grandpa died. I went into the streets with my friends and then Rosa, who was my best friend, was arrested and hanged. I found my mama and then the man who we stayed with started to beat her and call her terrible things." The tears streamed out. "I can't, Ollie. There's something wrong with me."

"Oh, Fae, there's nothing wrong with you," said Ollie. His face was broken as he reached out to her. "You don't need to hide."

"I do!" Fae's cry was a strangled, panicking thing. She took another step back. "I have to hide. If I don't hide, bad things happen. I'm wrong, Ollie. There's something terrible about me, something I have to keep away from other people." A fat sob choked her. "Even you."

"Don't say that, Fae." His voice was cracked.

"You know it's true. I've had to be hidden away my whole life," said Fae. "Mama hid me away. Grandma and Grandpa hid me away – it's just the way it is."

"It doesn't have to be."

"Yes, it does, Ollie! What's changed about me? What's made me different from when Grandma and Grandpa kept me hidden in the house?"

Ollie paused. His hand was still outstretched toward her, but the expression in his eyes had a depth of empathy and compassion to it that made Fae hesitate even though she wanted to run and run away and never come back.

"Nothing," he said softly.

"See?" Fae swallowed at her tears. "There is something wrong with me."

"No, Fae. There's nothing wrong with you." He came closer, holding out both of his hands. "There never was."

"Then why was I hidden away?"

"That had nothing to do with you," said Ollie. "It was all about the people who were hiding you."

"How can you know that?"

"Because I know you best." Ollie laughed through his tears. "I know you better than anyone, don't I? You were my friend, Fae. I came to find you every single time, no matter how hard you were trying to hide, remember?"

He pulled off his spectacles and tucked them into a back pocket; without them, the love in his eyes was bare and obvious.

"I won't stop you if you want to hide, Fae," he whispered. "But I want you to know that I'll always be one step behind you. I'll follow you no matter where you run, always waiting for you to turn around and come to me. I've waited six long years for you to come home to me. I've loved you for every second, even when I couldn't see you. I've searched for you and I'll keep searching for you for every moment of every day, no matter what." Ollie took a long breath. "Because I love you. And I always will. I want to show you to everyone I know because I think you're the most wonderful, beautiful, gentle person I've ever seen in my life."

Fae realized with stunned awareness that she was smiling. A half-laugh, half-sob fell from her mouth. He'd been holding on to that memory just the same as she had.

"I think you're interesting," she managed.

Ollie choked a little on his tears. "I think you're fascinating," he whispered. "So there."

He stepped forward, holding out his hands. She ran to him,

grasping both his hands, crying and laughing at the same time. Wrapping her in his arms, Ollie kissed her forehead again. "I won't show you to the whole town just yet, then," he whispered to her. "But can I show you to my brother?"

Fae smiled up at him. Love and terror clashed in her soul, but she saw in his eyes that love would win.

"A-all right," she murmured.

"Good," said Ollie. He took her hand. "Ready?"

"Ready," said Fae.

And she followed him forward, into her future.

CHAPTER 14

The trap rattled to a halt in the bustling streets, the fat cob snorting and shaking its head in concern at the amount of traffic buzzing around him.

"Easy, boy," said Otis, reining him in. "It's all right."

"He's not used to the city," said Myrtle, laughing as she held Otis' arm. "Truth be told, I know how he feels." She gazed at the tall buildings and busy streets around her, her eyes wide. "I've never been here before."

"Neither have I," said Otis, "but luckily Fae here is an old hand, isn't she?" He twisted around to smile kindly at Fae where she sat in the back seat. "You know your way around."

Ollie put an arm gently around Fae's shoulders, drawing her

protectively nearer to him. "And if we get lost, we have a map," he added.

Fae said nothing. It had been a year since she last saw these streets, but she remembered that the last time she came here, they had swallowed her up for six of the worst years of her entire life. The looming memory of that awful time towered over her, threatening to swallow up the joy that the last year had brought her.

"Are you ready, my love?" asked Ollie gently.

"I... I don't know," said Fae. She swallowed hard, the acrid scent of the city bringing back the suffering she'd endured there. "Maybe we should go back."

"We can if you want to," said Ollie, kissing her cheek. "But remember why we came here in the first place."

The fingers of Fae's right hand went to her left, touching the silver ring on her finger, feeling its smoothness. It was evidence that she wasn't just a lost orphan anymore. She looked up at Ollie, smiling. "We came here to find Peggy and Lucas."

"That's right, my darling." Ollie touched her cheek fondly. "You've done so well the last few months in the village, going out shopping at the market and making new friends – you can do this."

Fae intertwined her fingers with his. "I'm your wife," she said, hope filling her voice. "*We* can do this."

"Yes, we can." Ollie opened the door and climbed out, helping Fae down beside him. "We'll meet you at the inn tonight, Otis?"

"Of course," said Otis. "See you later." He cracked the whip, and the cob trundled off, spooking at some garbage cans.

"Are you all right, dear?" asked Ollie.

"I..." Fae looked around, dizzied by the crowds. "Everyone can see me," she whispered.

"That's right, and that's exactly how it should be." Ollie hugged her tightly. "You're the most beautiful creature in this whole city, remember?"

Her fear lost in love, Fae gazed up into his eyes. "You are so good to me, Ollie," she said. "I could never have wished for a better husband – or a better life back home." She laughed. "I still can't believe that Grandma and Grandpa left their farm to me."

"And I can't believe we never found that will in those old drawers," said Ollie, shaking her head. "But I'm so glad we finally did."

"I'm also glad you and Otis and Myrtle stayed," said Fae. "The farm is more than big enough for all four of us."

"And it's big enough for more." Ollie squeezed her hand. "That's why we're here, remember? To find those two little ones and bring them home."

Fae nodded, determined. "We'll give them the wonderful life you gave me." She bit her lip. "If we can find them."

She stared out at the enormous streets of London, running through the city like the veins of a great, filthy, predatory beast. It had swallowed her up and digested her in its festering belly for so long. How would they ever find two little children in this huge and terrible place?

Ollie seemed to sense her worry. He squeezed her fingers so that she looked up at him, then bent down to kiss her.

"Don't worry, Fae," he said, his eyes alight with adoration. "I spent my whole life searching for you. I'm good at finding things. And I don't give up. So, we won't either. Not until they're safe and living with us."

The End

CONTINUE READING...

Thank you for reading **The Invisible Daughter! Are you wondering what to read next?** Why not read **The Forsaken Maid's Secret? Here's a sneak peek for you:**

Bincy clung to her mother's hand as they moved through the street. Mama was walking quickly today; her scarf was pulled tightly around her throat, her hat low over her eyes, and Bincy had to hurry to keep up. Running made her chest burn a little, but she knew Mama had a reason for being in a hurry.

"Where are we going, Mama?" she asked, pausing to cough.

Mama looked down at her. Her mother's eyes had been blue once, but the pressure of hardship seemed to have squeezed the color out of them; now they were watery and gray, just like the weather.

"Just to buy something for dinner," she said, with a quick smile.

"Dinner?" Bincy's heart leapt. "Oh, that'll be nice, Mama. I'm so hungry."

"I know you are, darling." Mama sighed. She gave Bincy's arm a little tug. "You and all four of your siblings, just like you've been for the seven months since your papa…" She stopped.

"Why did he leave?" asked Bincy. "Where did he go?"

"I've told you and told you. Where he went, I don't know," said Mama shortly. "I don't want to know, either. And as for why he left, I suppose we were just one problem too many for him." Her voice was bitter.

Bincy held Mama's hand more tightly. "I'm sorry I made you sad."

"It's not your fault," said Mama with a long sigh.

"I'm not gonna think about him," said Bincy, trying to make her mother feel better. "Let's think about the nice dinner we're going to have soon. We're going to all sit and eat together, and it's going to be nice. We haven't had anything all day, but now we're all going to go to bed with full tummies."

To Bincy's surprise, a tear sneaked out of the corner of Mama's eye. She dashed it away quickly, but Bincy had seen it. "Why are you crying?" she asked, scared. The last time Mama had cried had been when Bincy's little brother, Jack, had died in the night. "Is someone dead?"

"No, no, my darling. Nothing like that," said Mama. "Hush now. Just hush and walk with me, there's a good girl."

Bincy obeyed, holding Mama's hand as they reached the outskirts of the slum where they lived. Everyone in the area had grown used to the smell; it was a strangely dynamic thing, changing every morning and every time the wind blew, alternately bringing whiffs in from the rotting Thames or the deep reek from the factories.

Visit Here to Continue Reading:

http://www.ticahousepublishing.com/victorian-romance.html

THANKS FOR READING

If you **love Victorian Romance, Click Here:**

https://victorian.subscribemenow.com/

to hear about all **New Faye Godwin Romance Releases! I will let you know as soon as they become available!**

Thank you, Friends! If you enjoyed *The Invisible Daughter!* would you kindly take a couple minutes to leave a positive review on Amazon? It only takes a moment, and positive reviews truly make a difference. Thank you so much! I appreciate it!

Much love,

Faye Godwin

MORE FAYE GODWIN VICTORIAN ROMANCES!

We love rich, dramatic Victorian Romances and have a library of Faye Godwin titles just for you! (Remember that ALL of Faye's Victorian titles can be downloaded FREE with Kindle Unlimited!)

VISIT HERE to discover Faye's Complete Collection of Victorian Romance:

https://ticahousepublishing.com/victorian-romance.html

ABOUT THE AUTHOR

Faye Godwin has been fascinated with Victorian Romance since she was a teen. After reading every Victorian Romance in her public library, she decided to start writing them herself —which she's been doing ever since. Faye lives with her husband and young son in England. She loves to travel throughout her country, dreaming up new plots for her romances. She's delighted to join the Tica House Publishing family and looks forward to getting to know her readers.

contact@ticahousepublishing.com

Printed in Poland
by Amazon Fulfillment
Poland Sp. z o.o., Wrocław